Waffling Bride

Book 2 in the Guardians, Inc. Series

L.B. Brookes

Like me on Instagram for delicious teasers, breaking release news and contests and giveaways:

https://www.instagram.com/l.b.brookes

Contents

Dedication

To Peggy- You're an inspiration and my favorite sister. I love all your superpowers. But some stand out more than others, like your intensity to fix things that matter and your loving heart to see the things that are worth the fight.

Acknowledgments

Brian- Thanks for being my partner in this crazy journey called life.

About the Author

L.B. Brookes writes contemporary romance novels that revolve around intrigue and danger. This danger brings everything to the surface. She likes sharing the excitement of her characters handling the emotions of falling in love while fighting for what is important to them. Good, bad, right, or wrong gets thrown into the mix while her characters become better versions of themselves. Love truly matters.

When L.B. Brookes is not writing, she is sailing on the Chesapeake Bay with her husband, family, and friends. When that isn't possible, she enjoys all forms of artwork, reading a good book, doting on her cat, and enjoying her coffee chats with friends at Fords.

L.B. Brookes enjoys hearing from her readers, so please send her an email at lbb@lbbrookes.com

Prologue

The leader of The Copperheads, Mr. Edward Sharpe, took off his pair of glasses and cleaned the lenses in a precise and articulate manner. Seated with impeccable posture, he commanded attention, he positioned himself front and center in the room. His demeanor radiating authority as he took center stage in the room. Every gesture and movement emphasized his dominance over those around him.

He made every posturing opportunity to substantiate his superiority over anyone else in attendance.

When the spectacles rested back on his face, he pivoted to his assistant and said, "It's warm in here, Daniels. Turn down the thermostat."

"I did, Sir. Before they all arrived, I placed it on its lowest temperature setting." Jennifer Daniels looked at the aging window unit as the mechanical fans whined and rattled, trying to keep the designated temperature below sixty-eight degrees.

"It's still warm," he pointed out. The drumming of his

fingertips against the table's surface indicated his want for an instant solution.

"I will order a free-standing unit after this session. Unfortunately, not being aware of today's meeting gave me little time to prepare properly."

"Daniels, your excuses are tiresome," he reprimanded. After that severe set-down, his attention switched to the others in the room, who all shifted in their seats and avoided making direct eye contact with him.

No one wanted Sharpe's... or Mr. Black's ire focused on them. People tended to disappear when that happened. It hadn't gone unnoticed by anyone that Miles Jennings wasn't the only one missing from today's meeting. The reasons for their absences stemmed from many gruesome rumors, none of which anyone wished to question.

"Now, before our latest guest arrives, I'll need an update on the new associates hired for the Freedman's compound. Mr. Black requested they have experience with children." Sharpe spoke in a soft voice, but his glare held an icy heaviness. Most in attendance skimmed his direct scrutiny by shuffling papers or adjusting their bodies in their seats. But an inundated amount of cleared throats and murmured assents followed.

It gave Edward immense pleasure to have all of them

uncomfortable. He understood the importance of instilling that emotion. Fear was an excellent motivator in his line of work.

However, to his continuing annoyance, Jennifer Daniels' face did not indicate having any feelings whatsoever. And every day since their first encounter, she was becoming more adept at showing less as the days passed.

Doing well to keep a neutral expression, Ms. Daniels took meeting minutes as Sharpe conducted the business at hand. Timetables and maintenance issues were discussed for Freedman's Village, West Point, and other facilities. Other topics of assignments and personnel sounded functional, under different conditions, even menial.

If not for the fact that all those matters discussed set plans in motion for an underground movement wanting to overthrow the Western Countries' governments.

At least to start.

But, I guess, like running any other business. You'd want to keep track of the bouncing balls. Any other of Jennifer's subsequent thoughts got interrupted when the door across the room opened.

Two guards yanked a man inside with a hood over his face with his hands cuffed behind his back.

"Place him beside my secretary. Daniels, pull a chair out for him," Edward Sharpe ordered.

After Jennifer did as directed, the guards forced the prisoner to sit. They had him leaning, almost off the seat, to release a wrist from behind him, only to refasten that cuff's loose end to the back of the chair and zip tie the freed wrist to the chair's arm.

Where do they think he is going to go? She silently scoffed.

One of the guards whipped off the man's hood and shoved the chair toward the table. The prisoner's chest pressed tight to the table edge. He looked quite the sight with the gag tied tight around the back of the head with his glasses askew.

Unable to resist, she gently corrected the frames to lie evenly across the bridge of his nose.

She was not at all surprised when that got her a look from Mr. Sharpe, who frowned upon anyone taking action without his specific direction. But what did, astonishingly enough, cause a jolt was the reaction from the man she just tried to help. Instead of showing gratefulness for the small kindness, he expressed disgust.

Like he saw a bug crawling underfoot.

Well, okay, see if I help you next time.

With mental shields fully erected, she figured her face must have somehow conveyed those thoughts because a slight lift of his lips peeked around the gag, and a blatant humor flashed into his eyes.

Huh… I guess this bug just got more interesting. No sooner, letting that thought escape, did Miss Daniels clear her throat, straighten her skirt, and settle back in the conference chair. The motto, 'Better the devil you know than the devil you don't,' sprung to mind, and she eased closer to Mr. Sharpe.

"Daniels, remove the gag," Sharpe ordered as his gaze returned to the new arrival. "Remember, I am immune to your special ability. Any attempt to influence others with your persuasion power will have your son punished."

A few of Sharpe's associates knew he had quite a strong talent with mind manipulation, too, but only if his touch partnered the attempts.

Jennifer got up immediately. With the cloth tied so tightly, she feared hurting him while loosening the knot.

"Mr. McKnight, My name is Edward Sharpe. These are my associates." He waved a hand, encompassing the people around the table. "I'll make introductions of a few of them later."

The new arrival remained quiet. But his face reflected a heavy layer of distrust.

"Come now, Andrew- You are among admirers. No person is more qualified to write this book for us than you!"

"Lucky me," Mr. McKnight said. His voice coated in sarcasm.

"Yes. Yes, you are. Suppose you keep an open mind. Isn't that what journalists and political historians need when they brilliantly write as you have in the past?"

"It's hard to be open-minded when cuffed to a chair, and you threaten my son."

"Of course! Guards, take them off immediately. From now on, have care with Mr. McKnight."

One guard came forward to unlock the restraints.

"Understand, any foolishness on your part will have the restraints returned," Sharpe warned.

Andrew slowly eased his arms to the front, massaging their stiffness, and then did the same for his hands. While brooding over the room's occupants, Andrew counted ten, including himself. Everyone was dressed in fine business suits like they were attending an executive board meeting. His political knowledge as a commentator and author allowed him to recognize two of the many faces surrounding him. Their long life in politics meant that their identities were frequently broadcasted on numerous news channels throughout the week.

What they were doing with his captors, Andrew had no clue.

And, of course, the lone woman who sat beside him caught his attention. Although seemingly appearing like a quiet little thing with kind, big, crystal-blue eyes, Andrew suspected otherwise. *A puzzle, to be sure.*

"We took care of the first part of today's business, so most of you can go. Those of you I spoke to before the meeting remain seated.

"Mr. Green, make Mr. Black aware of today's events. Let us know when you successfully insert yourself within the investigation and have access to Maxwell.

"Daniels-"

"Of course," Jennifer said while pushing back the chair to leave.

"No, Daniels. Stay."

The majority of the room emptied. Two other men stayed seated besides Mr. McKnight, Mr. Sharpe, and his assistant. Mr. Sharpe waved his hand to them and said, "These men are going to help-"

"Sharpie-"

"Call me Edward."

"Sharpie, it is hard for me to write a book about a group of vigilantes who have kidnapped my son and myself. If you had approached me on the up and up, I would have found this intriguing and possibly would have agreed. But now... we'll never know, will we?"

"Exactly–it is unfortunate that matters got handled, as you said. But it is too important. It's easier to beg forgiveness than ask permission."

"Oh, is that what you're doing here, begging for forgiveness? And what's to stop you from killing my son and me once I finish the book? Or if you don't like what I have written?"

"All these concerns will go away once you know our cause better. Hasn't your stay with us shown our good faith? Hasn't Thomas enjoyed our kind hospitality?" Sharpe's eyebrows rose, and the glint in his eyes flashed back to their typical piercing coldness.

Swiveling in his chair, Sharpe surveyed the room's other occupants. "I have asked the two men with us today to gather details about our organization. They will be available to gather any additional information you feel is required." Sharpe gestured with a hand toward the back of the room. "Mr. Davis and Mr. Thompson, can you take the boxes of files out to the van?"

"What happens if I read your supplied material and still

disagree with you?"

"That won't happen. Once you read the material, you will support us. Don't you want your son to have a brighter future?" Mr. Sharpe was undaunting in this belief.

"And if you're wrong?"

Uh-oh… I know the answer to that one. But outwardly, Jennifer's demeanor gave nothing away as to those inner thoughts.

Mr. Sharpe cleared his throat before replying, "We aren't wrong, Andrew." His gesturing for the two men hesitating in the middle of the room to leave made them depart in great haste.

"Daniels-"

"Why do you call her that?" Andrew asked.

"What—her name?" Mr. Sharpe laughed, dismissing the question.

"You call everyone in this room, Mr. Green, Mr. Black, Mr. Davis, and so on, but her just Daniels. Is it because of her rank, role, or gender?"

Mr. Sharpe paused, not used to people questioning his methods or answering to them, with the exception of Mr. Black. And even then, Sharpe found ways to skirt those directives.

Jennifer glared at the back of Andrew McKnight's head and

became confounded as Andrew suddenly pivoted. His gaze pierced hers with a searching intensity.

Does he still see me as just a bug or another vile species altogether? She wondered.

How about more like a butterfly? Came through loud and clear in her mind.

As Andrew's comment pierced through solid shields, Jennifer barely held back a gasp. Her facial expression remained neutral, but a recitation of basic multiplication tables started in her thoughts.

The minutes slowly ticked by as these two opponents battled for control.

Mr. Sharpe's reply postponed their silent war. "Daniels will be helping you with your book. And I call her Daniels because of her role." His chin jerked upward before he added, "Satisfied, Andrew?"

The captive writer shrugged with a preoccupied hesitation. His gaze remained locked on Jennifer Daniels.

"But-" Jennifer inserted. Caught off guard with this new directive, she quickly added, "Sir, what about my work with you?"

"You'll stay with me for the most part, but on Thursday

afternoons, you'll leave for the other facility, work with Andrew through the weekend, and be back here Monday 0800. (8:00 a.m.)"

"Aren't your fellow thugs allowed to have a life?" Andrew commented.

"Unfortunately, in any case, sacrifices must be made," Mr. Sharpe pointed out.

"So, you work on the weekends as well?"

Mr. Sharpe adjusted his glasses and stood up, not bothering to give Andrew a reply.

"Sir. It won't be a problem," Ms. Daniels hurriedly intervened and sent Mr. McKnight a look with fierce eyes and a clenched jaw. *Knock it off.* She shot out telepathically.

"The guards will escort you out." Sharpe gestured with his hand for the men to come forward.

Andrew stood up at their approach.

Springing out of the chair and gathering her belongings, Jennifer started to leave.

Andrew blocked her escape with a slight shift in his stance. "Mr. Sharpe, if I give my word to go quietly with the guards, can Ms. Daniels accompany me to the van? I can give her detailed instructions on what I will need to start the process."

Sharpe nodded his head before going through the doorway. "You have fifteen minutes," he ordered his assistant as he left.

With a smirk, Andrew addressed the guards, "Carry on, boys. The clock is ticking for Ms. Daniels." He brought his hands around to the back, and the restraints were quickly fastened again.

"Can we go without the hood? It is quite hot," Andrew said to the closest guard.

"I can help with that," Jennifer said, reaching into an enormous canvas bag almost half her size. With a slight delay, a pair of scissors was retrieved by moving a few items around in the cavernous void. She began cutting into Andrew's shirt and dissecting the seam that joined the sleeve to the shoulder yoke. Her fingers brushed along the torn edge of his sleeve and unbuttoned the cuff at the wrist.

Andrew shivered when the sharp edge of the scissors cut along the length of his arm. The fabric hung loose and became easy to pull away from his restraints. His gaze followed her hands, and everything turned blurry when she gently took off his glasses and tucked them into his breast pocket.

With Jennifer's fuzzy form completing some unknown tasks, Andrew stood waiting. Only when she approached him again, holding out an arm-length piece of folded fabric did he anticipate the next difficulty and bent forward.

Just before the blindfold blocked any further visuals, her face became more focused, and he stared intently into those deep beautiful blue eyes.

She trembled and hastily broke any further connection with the thin pieces of fabric.

"Cold?" Andrew asked.

Jennifer didn't like how her body reacted to his presence. "No, of course not," she said, starting to tie the knot. "It's-" She jerked the cloth tighter. "Hot-" Another more forceful tug followed. "In here," Jennifer concluded while securing the binding around his head and lightly tapping the blindfold in place.

"Many thanks... I'm finding myself slightly cooler," he replied, swiveling around and raising his arm. Andrew continued, "Do you mind holding onto me, Ms. Daniels? It's hard to keep one's balance without sight."

His curved lips, heavy with amusement, briefly distracted her before a pulsating attack immediately followed when she took hold of Andrew's bare arm. *You will walk out with me, distract the guards, and help me escape!*

The deeply mesmerizing thoughts of Andrew McKnight

caressed her mind. A warmth encompassed her whole being causing numerous disturbing effects within her body. None of which, however, gave her the urge to do as he commanded.

"Okay, Mr. McKnight." Not wanting him to try his thing on the guards and get them both in trouble, Jennifer swiftly pulled up on the discarded rag still looped around his neck and reapplied the gag. She switched her hold onto the other arm, fully covered by his shirt, to lead him out of the room.

Hate to break it to you, Andrew. Jennifer telepathically replied to his compulsion attempt. *But it isn't working on me.*

Andrew didn't bother disclosing that his mind control usually only worked when spoken out loud. Or, did he want to add–the more unsettling discovery–that she was the first person who could telepathically communicate with him. So, it had seemed prudent to give it a try.

After all, he would do anything to get Tommy and himself out of this mess.

Chapter One

As the young woman slowly blinked open her eyes, she found herself greeted by the gentle embrace of the late morning sun. These rays filtered through the draperies, bathing the room in a golden glow. The curtains, adorned with delicate eyelet and embroidered patterns, danced gracefully in the breeze that flowed through the slightly opened windows. Her tumbled hair fell around her head on the pillow in a deep-chestnut-colored halo. A faint, pink-colored blush highlighted one visible cheek as the opposing side of her face burrowed into a downy softness. Her lips moved, grazing along the skin of her hand, tucked under her cheek that pressed into the pillow.

Having slept so warm and snug, Allison Maxwell was reluctant to wake up.

A yawn spread across her face in sleepy increments. Allowing the small smile to form seemed too much of an effort, and snuggling into the solid warmth nearby became the next natural thing for her to do.

A faint, strange dream about her uncle began to take shape and tug at her memory. His message didn't make sense, with the jumbled content refusing to come together. Suspecting its importance, she tried to bring it to the surface.

But like a movie trailer tripped to roll, clips of recent events reeled through Allison's mind instead. Fear, taking hold, made a loud gasp escape as her body lost its relaxed pose. The shadowy terrorist group wanting to do her harm slammed front and center on her list of concerns.

As she froze in place, the flight response was gearing up for action.

She would have stuttered if anyone had asked her a week ago if she could spur anyone's vengeful actions. Maybe even joked, "Would selecting the wrong granite for a client's kitchen count?" Although, the rapid-firing memories of what happened yesterday would provide a different response today.

Scenes that fit precisely at home in the many action-packed movies that she and her sister, Peggy, loved to watch would say differently. But even those silly heroines didn't stupidly pull off antics as she had pulled last night.

Sara! Allison cringed. *What had I been thinking?*

A mental tallying of those mistakes came screeching to a full stop. That 'cherry on top' of a melting sundae of her messed-up life stood front and center, prompting Allison to push out from under the covers. The flight response finally kicked in.

But she didn't get far. Startled, she whipped around.

A metal cuff on Allison's slim wrist tethered to someone else had halted further motion. And while her heart thumped erratically in her chest, she cried out in remembered outrage.

All the recently compiled grievances, her unwilling, protective stalemate leading to the loss of her normal, carefree life, getting on several small planes when suffering from Aerophobia, and getting drugged twice, could be laid at HIS feet.

Lastly, and most outrageous of them all, was that THAT MAN, the responsible individual, William Maxwell, her ex-boyfriend– aka, the cherry on top–could now be called something else.

Her husband.

With Allison's sudden movements, Will's eyes shot open, and he rubbed his face with his free hand, releasing a wide yawn. Having been awake since hearing her gasp, he prepared for a fight.

She tried pulling away. "Did you have me handcuffed all night?!"

"A lot of shit went down yesterday. So yeah, I did," Will said. As he spread his arms above his head, flexing into a slow stretch, a realization came rushing to the forefront.

Amazing things came out of it, too. My daughter, Sara, for one.

A glance at Will's custom watch lying on the bedside table confirmed they slept late. After tossing and turning in a bed down the hall for an hour or so last night, the decision became apparent to him: *Why not just go to the source of my problems?*

Which, of course, proved correct. Only after lying beside Allison, listening to her relaxed breathing, did Will finally recognize the other fantastic gift.

A gift that he wasn't willing to return. So, wanting to talk to his waffling bride this morning, he did this one small thing before surrendering to sleep. And he truly had used the cuffs so that she couldn't avoid him if she woke before him.

She certainly had put Will through hell yesterday in fleeing a massive avoidance–more like a three-year lie. He wouldn't put it past her to attempt another disappearing act.

Maneuvering Allison exactly where he wanted her, he wouldn't blow the opportunity given to him for all the money in the world. The hard part would be convincing Allison to follow his lead. And not just with the investigation or with Sara.

But with matters of the heart as well.

Presently annoyed, she looked like she'd take a swing at him to accompany that fiery glare. In Will's opinion, this became a satisfying by-product.

However, some of its impact got lost, with only one of her witch-hazel eyes–now a deep, forest green–remained hidden with most of her features behind the wavy, disarray of hair surrounding her slim, oval-shaped face.

But what he saw still successfully translated the flash of ire as her one arm–linked with his–got pulled along with his stretching movements. Adding insult to injury was accommodating her petite frame to his much larger one.

Her free hand swept away the tumbled mess from her face, which made it all the more possible to show a full-frontal assault of flashing eyes, naturally pink, full-shaped lips, and flush-colored cheeks his way.

What honest man could sympathize with her predicament when the result gave him this visual reaction?

Definitely not Will.

He took his sweet time finding the key and unlocking his and her wrist, grinning at her outraged face. His positive frame of mind had more to do with his resolved feelings for Allison than catching up on sleep. He leaned in closer and gave her a swift kiss on the lips. "How did you sleep?" he asked, shifting away to put on his wrist device now that the cuffs were off.

Allison sputtered.

Finding him bare-chested, unshaven, and looking incredibly handsome in her bed was one thing. But his gorgeous body, stretched out and on display while grinning and kissing her, became something else entirely.

Keeping an openly cheerful expression in place, Will returned, pushed her back down among the pillows, and shifted onto his side. Inclining over her, moving his one unclothed, muscular leg, he successfully pinned her in place. "Now, let's just relax, Allison," he coaxed.

Too unsettled to provide better mental shields, Allison broadcasted loud and clear in his head. *Yeah, right, like that's going to happen.* She silently scoffed.

"It can," Will promised. His telepathic ability quickly picked up her thoughts. "We need to get a few things straight. Mmm?"

His exhaled breath tickled her left ear as he got even closer.

He is–too much! Came screaming into Will's head. "Yes, I am," he replied, shifting his tactile exploration toward Allison's neck.

Anticipation had him grinning when her head whipped around to block his wandering lips. And this instantly gave him what he had wanted all along. "Are you comfortable, Ally?" he whispered a few inches from her lips.

To have faced him head-on became a big mistake.

She found her breathing becoming irregular and willed herself to be unaffected. But her flushed face and eyes expressed numerous emotions: rebellion, fear, and longing.

He forced a slight chuckle when anything but humor battled his purpose. Allison's nearness also began clouding his focus. His long, muscular limb slowly moved away, ensuring his movement caressed her bare legs. His slow retreat provided a direct attack on her senses.

Allison's eyes narrowed to a stern glare. But her trembling told another story, and a vulnerability flickered across her beautiful face. "Is this your revenge, Will? Using this attraction against me?"

"Revenge? Isn't that a little dramatic?" Will tilted his head to the side with glittering specks highlighted in his golden-brown eyes. "But what would you call it when leaving a federal officer stranded in that diner's parking lot to run from my protection and fly petrified across the country?

"Not to mention keeping a three-year secret as you did." His teeth nipped softly on her jawline.

"What?" she hesitated, clearly confused. By all accounts, Will deserved to be mad. He clearly had no problem showing his anger yesterday. But now, he looked relaxed, sounding playful.

Advancing closer when she stayed tongue-tied, he teased, "Have you developed a dramatic flair since we stopped being lovers?"

Wetting her lips with her tongue, she regretted it when it drew Will's attention. "Umm..." A barely there voice kept Will's gaze intent. They remained glued to those soft, rounded contours that now glistened with moisture.

Leaning in closer, he almost touched her lips. "Let's get an answer another way," he said before closing the mere gap between their mouths. The kiss instantly swept them both over.

Will's best friend would have a surfing term to name the occurrence, but he didn't care at the moment.

Falling into the long spiral ride of pleasurable sensations and the eruption of heat, Will had always had the power to shut off her mind and make her want oblivion. Allison went willingly into the madness. She pulled him closer, craving the weight of him.

Caught in a trap of his own making, Will didn't want to pull free. He reacquainted himself with every rounded contour and valley of her body while reminding her how good they were together with caressing touches and teasing strokes. For many moments, the sounds of their mutual passions filled the room before Will fought to get control of his desires.

Her tantalizing smell.

Her soft skin.

Her eager touch.

Drove him on within the vortex of fast-beating hearts, dizzying pleasures, and unrelenting sensual cravings.

But he wanted–no, needed–it to be her decision. Not his coercion. So with tremendous effort, his kisses softened, his hands soothed, while whispering loving promises each time his lips touched hers.

Carefully pulling them back from the brink, he knew too much was riding on this.

Sex was giving into just another bodily function if the heart's proclamation got left out, and he wanted to commit the shit out of what he and Allison had. And what they had wasn't just a physical connection.

Will understood that now. But Allison needed to reach that same conclusion.

So, they must wait for a better time to consummate yesterday's legal union.

Chapter Two

With the easing of Will's seductive explorations came the flaring misgivings of Allison's thoughts surfacing once more, prompting her to pull away.

That was what she did when things got too serious. And Will made her forget why it became crucial to maintain that distance.

Not that she wanted to, but it had become second nature now.

Having been taught that people got killed if they got too close to the Buchanan family and quite accustomed to severe loss at a young age, over and over, she tended to avoid letting people in.

A nudging memory of her uncle's bedside warnings tried to resurface again, but she drove it back down. The need to sharpen her survival instincts for this present predicament took all she had at the moment.

Will eased from their embrace, too. Quickly rolling onto his back he said, "I don't want you to regret what happened, Allison." His heart rate, equally affected, struggled for normalcy. Coping with his body's primal reaction proved difficult. His body vibrated with wanting to claim her.

He reached for a pillow to tuck behind his head while watching her pull the duvet to cover up herself.

Allison's vulnerability helped settle him back to normal. Or close to it. Something needed to be said, but he wasn't sure how to go about it. Since logic still struggled against his physical needs.

But then, the perfect opening presented itself.

"What now?" Her voice held a slight tremble.

He became very alert but conscious of his body language, trying to stay loose and casual. The same way, when settling an easily spooked client required him to pull from his wheelhouse of tricks. But knowing this particular skill set wasn't his strongest, he upped his game.

"We stay married and raise Sara together," Will said while reaching into her thoughts, gauging her reaction–determined to find the right words to say.

The surprise nearly had his body jolting. Allison's ability to keep her thoughts private immediately blocked and shoved him completely out.

How interesting.

Allison turned to stare at him as if he had two heads. "Did you take a knock to the head recently? Yesterday, you found out that you have a daughter. That I've kept from you. You forced me into a wedding by stealing control of my daughter, and I'm supposed to believe-"

"I know." Will leaned in, his eyes glinting sparks of urgency. "Ally, I was furious yesterday."

It was more like fear morphing into anger because that was how he managed that emotion. "Hell, it came as quite a shock to find out we have a daughter. Not to mention the damn stunt you pulled evading Jeff and leaving the safe house," Will explained.

"But you want... us?" Allison interceded, her voice lowered to a whisper.

Will's head immediately nodded before saying, "Last night, I had a chance to look at it from your perspective. You weren't the only one who made mistakes, you know." Eye contact snapped off her for a mere second before returning.

He took a deep breath before his words poured out in a rushed confession. "I should have understood your response back then. The history with your uncle, your first husband, and then Nancy's interference certainly did not help matters. Hell, I used it as a buffer for my own reasons.

"You were right." Will reached for Allison's hand and held on before continuing, "My attempts to explain were half-hearted."

"Then why didn't you-" Allison couldn't say it.

"Come back sooner?" Will finished for her. His gaze implored as the hands holding her tightened. "Ally, I fell so hard for you. Like never before–not even with Rachael. There is this strong... link. An unbreakable connection. I didn't trust how rapidly that happened. I just jumped at the chance to relocate. To get distance from it."

Will's final admission on why he took Senator Buchanan's plea of maintaining Allison's protection from afar stood out like a beacon. His need to keep her safe was just as strong if not more than her uncle's. And when a viable threat appeared, like Nancy's Copperhead henchmen, that need went ballistic.

The urge to confess his company's involvement with her shadowed security details over the past years weighed heavy on his conscience. But a persistent doubt stood in the way. Would she understand? Or would Allison use the information to pull further away from him?

One hand reached out to cup her cheek. His thumb brushed along the contours of her lips, caressing the softness. "My regret came instantaneously. But I'm stubborn." He chuckled before continuing, "So, of course, I fought it even more."

His fingers stroked along her jaw line before dropping to the bedspread. A frustrated shrugging of his shoulders ended with a heavy sigh. "I was in DC, doing what I thought I loved doing, but something was missing.

"I think I was destined to love you," he softly admitted. "I just didn't want to realize it. Or the power I felt you may have over me."

"No-" Allison shook her head in denial. What came out of Will's mouth was so unlike him.

He didn't speak of destiny... or admit to vulnerabilities.

She pulled her hands away. "You're wrong." She scooted off the bed, spotting her robe on the hook. Not at all surprised to be in the set of pajamas Will had dressed her in when he first brought her to the safe house.

Was it only a week ago that this whole mess started?

Her head shook to dispel that realization. She hastily covered herself and began moving. "I knew... you would do this."

"Do what?" Will watched as she paused in her frantic pacing.

"This-" Her finger pointed toward him, then to herself.

"I'm not following you." Will combed his fingers through his already disheveled, almost black-colored hair. Something he tended to do when he got agitated. His golden-brown eyes squinted while his gaze grew unfocused. His attempt to read her mind got blocked yet again.

"We barely talk or see each other for over three years and- And then... BAM! You have feelings for me and want to stay married!" A quick shake of her head accompanied a sharp tug on her robe's ties. "Not buying it! This is because of Sara. I get it; you want to have your daughter. But after-" Allison waved her hands, encompassing the space around them while adding, "this is finished. Your investigation is over, and we don't have to stay married."

Will laughed in relief. Her rousing emotions allowed a break in her mental shields. He saw her fears and knew what hurdles to overcome. "What a line of bull. When have you seen me do anything I didn't want to do?" He got out of bed and stood before her in just his boxer shorts, hands resting on his hips.

"You have a daughter now! You may be thinking of her and not-"

"Allison, you're not making sense. This family curse is not real!"

"It is!" Her brain was close to short-circuiting with his near-nakedness and the view of a certain body-part that tented under the light covering. She quickly commanded, "Get some clothes on!"

He released an exasperated groan. His eyes rolled up while open palms, fingers outstretched, got thrown outward, shaking in frustration. Quickly grabbing his pants, he roughly put them on, leaving the fastener undone. His erection refused to go quietly.

"Where does my uncle fit in all this? Is he coming here?" Allison asked, frowning. A foggy memory of talking to her uncle in an odd dream, surfaced again. His message about Will made sense; her uncle had always approved of her connection with Guardians Inc.'s CEO, but everything else didn't.

"I don't want my uncle involved in my life or my daughter's. If you still have a connection to him regarding your position with the FBI, that's just too bad." The fear of Senator Buchanan's powerful, outstretched control of her life in the past out shadowed the strange yet affectionate scene during a drug-induced sleep. She couldn't take the chance that her longings played out in a fanciful notion.

Will's direct connection to her uncle was severed last night. Guardians, Inc. no longer held Allison's security contract through her uncle. But Senator Buchanan had other ways to keep tabs on his ward.

"Unfortunately, he is on a committee that gets updates about the FBI's investigation. He was made aware of the cluster fuck in Florida yesterday. At first, he wanted to meet Sara. Now, the meeting is about the case.

"Your uncle holds no power over me, Allison. But I should tell you something." Will rubbed his face several times with the palm of his hand wondering if he should disclose what he was thinking. It was time to come clean.

The buzzing of the phone on the nearby table disrupted them. Will swiftly made his way to the house phone, his hand darting toward the flashing red button as he grasped the receiver. "What!" he barked. When a few moments passed with a murmured voice speaking on the other end, he sighed like the weight of the world pressed down on him. "Yeah?" he said, nodding his head up and down. "Understood. I'll be down shortly," he replied, stealing a glance at Allison.

The receiver got placed back on its base, and Will positioned his hands on his hips. "That was Pete, one of my men. There's a report that came in for Jeff and me to respond to," Will explained.

Allison released a deep, long breath. "What time is it? I need a shower."

Will glanced at his specialized wrist device that gave him the time as well as providing other unique features. "It's going on 9:30. Is Sara usually up by now?"

"Not if she can help it. She's usually asleep for another hour at least. With everything going on, that could change. Is she close?"

"Yeah, right across the hall," he replied as he cautiously approached. He dropped a brief kiss on her lips. He headed for his shirt on the nearby chair and said, "Go shower. I'll go check on her and meet you downstairs." Pulling on a T-shirt and buttoning his jeans–his body finally on board with his decision– he got ready to check on his daughter.

My daughter, man! What an awesome day. He decided.

Will began to whistle–his assurance in the resolution of what just transpired–reflected in his jolly tune.

Allison froze, her hand squeezed tighter on the bathroom's doorknob when those iconic notes reached her ears. With her mother's Southern roots, she easily recognized the 'Dixieland' song. "The South lost!" Allison shouted in annoyance.

If Will was counting on that anthem to spur his victory, it might lead to a defeat similar to those experienced by the Southern States. Setting aside her Southern heritage and the empathy she felt for what her country endured in the last Civil War–she wanted his capitulation.

She slammed the door closed, wanting to escape his cocky demeanor.

Not wanting to dwell on anything they discussed, Allison rushed through her shower and quickly dressed for the day.

Needing that shield of the armory for further interactions with Will made donning a light covering of make-up necessary.

But the importance of getting the right balance with numerous products took longer than she thought. Not to mention soothing her out-of-control emotions with each discovery of what Will got right when making sure she had everything she needed.

When the face in the mirror reflected a confidence she was nowhere near feeling it was time to go. Allison styled her still-damp hair into a low ponytail and left the bedroom.

A glance into the room across the hall found it empty. Allison swiftly left and headed to the guard at the top of the stairs. With her hasty approach, he pointed downward before she could speak.

Her daughter's laughter grew louder as Allison approached the bottom landing.

Sara had always adjusted to different and new developments better than her mother.

In fact, her daughter thrived on them. Allison's head shook in bemusement. Why would today be any different?

Looking forward to hugging her pint-sized, whirling dervish, she crossed the great room, reaching the massive, stone-topped countertop with custom millwork cabinets. The island separated the ample open space from the kitchen. Allison arrived just in time to witness FBI's Special Agent (GS-14) and Will's best friend, Jeffrey Collins, plucking Sara off the counter and twirling her around in a slow spin.

Will stood by the stove, holding a spatula, cooking. The delicious aroma wafting from the kitchen stirred Allison's appetite, causing her stomach to growl in anticipation of a meal. Will hadn't lost his culinary skills if it tasted half as good as it smelled.

With his child's laughter flowing, Will swung toward the sound just in time to catch Allison's appearance. The smile he sent her way while brushing aside a stray lock of his hair hit her heart with lethal intent.

Taking in his incredible physique–a walking contradiction to a typical computer nerd–Allison's brain switched off. Those rolled up sleeves to Will's button-down shirt revealed toned arms, making her treacherous eyes soak it all in with all the rest of him. His faded, well-worn, blue jeans hugged his waist and well-defined legs. The low-riding motorcycle boots gave him a badass vibe, illuminating his true personality.

A computer genius and Guardians, Inc. owner who had the look of a warrior.

Oh, my. How can anyone resist that? Allison's unguarded thought popped into Will's mind. His smile morphed into a wide grin as he said out loud, "Don't resist." His confidence coating every word.

Allison saw someone happy with what life had dished out and not opposed to fudging the details to suit his needs better.

Plus, their tangible presence wrapped her in a warm, heated embrace.

Liking the sensation so much, she didn't want to break free. *Wasn't it what I had wished for all those lonely nights?*

But the worry of what was at stake overshadowed everything else. It wasn't possible to be a family, so she didn't see the reason to pretend. What else would alter?

She fretted about their future. Besides the physical threat from the Sons of Liberty, there were other concerns. More than Allison's and her daughter's hearts stood on the line if things didn't work out between Will and her. Allison feared it may be too late to go back to what Sara's life was like before yesterday. Her uncle, knowing Sara's true parentage, came with complications.

Going over to her, Will softly kissed her and then backed away. "Everything will be fine," he said softly for her ears only.

But an immediate thought came through from Allison into his mind.

How can you be so sure?

"Because I'll do everything in my power to make it happen," he vowed. For once in Will's life, his response became reactionary.

Not calculated, studying it from several angles.

Nor weighed for the pros and cons tally.

No, he didn't care about the best course forward because this overwhelming compulsion came from that hidden, dark part of his psyche that didn't show itself often.

He knew then what he could become, what havoc he could unleash onto the world. To keep his family safe, he would do anything. There were no lines he wouldn't cross, and it wouldn't be pretty should any harm come to his family.

Chapter Three

In the bustling office of the FBI's Washington D.C. headquarters, the shrill ring of a phone pierced the air, drawing the attention of Agent Rebecca Patterson (GS-5) at her desk.

It was one of many ringing phones that had to be answered during her lunch break–due to the receptionist calling in sick. In this male-dominated field, she had a hard enough time reminding them of her investigation and ass-kick abilities than losing any ground as the backup administrative personnel–as if she preferred anything about office work.

She'd take a gun over a file, phone, or keyboard any day. And thanks to growing up with four season-hardened military brothers, she was an excellent shot.

"Hello, Federal Bureau of Investigations, Agent Patterson speaking," she answered while chewing a fresh bite of a smoked turkey and Swiss on rye.

"Take a coffee break with that sandwich, cross the street, and bring your cell phone." The male's voice hinted at an unfriendly get-together.

Agent Patterson's back went up as her sandwich slowly

lowered to meet its other half still placed on the white, wax-papered wrapping. She flung the long braid of her auburn-colored hair off one shoulder. "I'd like nothing better-"

The male caller didn't allow her to make a bad-ass comment back. "I hear you're close to being awarded Dinda's adoption papers; I can tell you there is a major problem preventing that. We can discuss this when we meet in ten minutes. Don't keep me waiting."

After the caller hung up, she pulled her gun out of the front drawer and looked around the busy room while securing it in its holster. She picked up her cell phone as her eyes scanned the crowded office.

Her slim, tall frame cut swiftly through the office as she hurriedly made her way to the exit. Looking confused and panicked–like a mother who got a call from the principal's office regarding her child–Rebecca hid her true feelings.

But a 'Cheshire's Cat' smile would have better suited her mood.

After receiving the information from her brother's team, she was beginning to think they wouldn't make contact. With her mind racing, she pushed the door with a substantial force.

About damn time.

****

A child's delightful giggle broke the spell between the newlyweds.

Sara was enjoying the extra attention she was receiving.

Being surrounded by new faces should keep an active and

bright-minded child entertained for a day or two.

Allison dragged her gaze back to Sara.

Only time would tell if the abrupt switch in her daughter's familial situation will trigger an epic crash. A three-year-old's meltdown wasn't a pretty sight and still a possibility.

After all, they did unexpectedly pull a three-year-old away from a fun-filled vacation at 'The Happiest Place on Earth.' Plus, even with assurances of their continuing assistance, they left behind Peggy and Bob.

They were on their own. A burst of air pushed out from Allison's lungs.

Sara held tight to Special Agent Jeffrey Collins' side with her tiny legs hooked around his waist. By the looks of it, he was swiftly becoming her newest idol.

Putting on a sunny smile, Allison greeted her daughter, "Well, it seems like someone is enjoying herself."

"I am going to be a pilot!"

"Ah, well-" Allison's mouth went as dry as a desert, and her heart stopped beating for several seconds. "That's super," she choked out, trying to sound encouraging. The thought of her baby flying on–let alone piloting a plane–made her want to shudder violently.

Jeff softly chuckled as he brought Allison into a loose embrace using his free arm. "You have a way to go before getting used to it, Mom."

"I have to work on that, don't I?"

Everyone at this point was clearly in the loop of Allison's

flying phobia.

"Not on my account. I prefer water over air, myself." He shifted slightly to glance at Will, who landed Jeff with Surfer as a nickname–due to the pro-surfing days spent in his youth and the love of spouting surfing lingo every chance he got. "I'm sure it will be handy for others, though."

Her gaze went to his sparkling blue eyes and dropped to the smirk around his mouth. Catching on to Jeff's meaning, Allison's attention pulled away from his sandy-blonde scruff, covering the jawline–due to not shaving in a couple of days. She elbowed him in the ribs.

"Ouch! Rough, too. I think I'm in love." Jeff tugged her closer.

Allison's laugh spilled out, relaxed and sincere. So thankful that her exploits yesterday didn't ruin their budding friendship. Her husky bubbles of sound floated around the room, falling pleasantly on the occupants' ears.

Adjusting her attention to her daughter, she missed Jeff's mischievous smile thrown at Will, who had eyes only for his bride.

Wipe out. Jeff sent to Will through their link.

The sound of grease popping in the pan had Will returning to the stove, sidetracking the cutting response he wanted to give back to his hilarious friend's telepathic ribbing.

"Hey… pretty girl. Are you having a good time?" Allison smiled at her daughter, already knowing the answer.

Sara bobbed her head enthusiastically. "Yes, Auntie, Mommy! Look, I'm a princess."

Yes, indeed. Allison's thought agreed, smiling and nodding. Fiercely loving her daughter didn't alter the fact that getting Sara dressed in the morning could prove difficult. The princess's outfit was an easy choice. Wait until he tried regular clothes–like shorts and a top–to see how quickly tantrums developed.

But no worries today because this outfit clearly checked off all her daughter's boxes. Sara's soft blue dress, the color of the sky–just before sunset–perfectly matched her eyes. A white, frilly, ruffle accent trimmed the bottom, and a broad, black-satin ribbon wrapped around her waist.

Not only did Sara get fully dressed, but her shining, black hair–clearly her father's daughter–was neatly combed back and adorned with two small butterfly barrettes.

"Well, I must agree. You look like you stepped out of one of our bedtime stories," Allison commented while admiring her daughter's appearance. Whoever tied the bow in the back did an awe-inspiring job. The position laid just right, with broad and full displaying loops. A pair of pristine white cotton socks with tiny blue ribbons weaved in at the edges finished the ensemble.

"Which one? Which one?!" Sara giggled.

As this was a favorite game between them, Allison jumped in, saying, "Hmmm, Let me think." She played along with a hand cupping her cheek with the forefinger tapping lightly against her face. "Which one of your favorite princesses has black hair? Snowy white complexion? Rosy red lips? Pretty ruffled dress and-"

"The shoes! Don't forget the shoes!" Sara embellished her

point by kicking out her legs, preening at her pretty feet.

Like her mother, Sara loved shoes; these were the prettiest, shiniest, and most adorable black-colored, Mary Jane shoes Allison had ever seen. They even had a jeweled buckle around the ankle that would make any little girl feel like royalty.

"Yes, I agree. I can't forget those gorgeous shoes," Allison said while studying Sara's footwear in great interest. "Hey! Do you think I can borrow them?"

Sara giggled in response.

Allison jokingly grabbed for the shoes while Jeff, a quick study, backed up and blocked her every attempt. Sara laughed even harder before saying, "Auntie... Play the game!"

"Okay. Okay, Your Highness. Let's see. Where were we?"

Sara yelled in excitement, "My shoes!"

"Yes, that's right, your darling shoes... Hmmm? How about Cinderella?" Allison guessed, and Sara quickly shook her head from side to side. "Sleeping Beauty?" Again, she met with the wrong answer. Allison puckered her face in concentration. "Ahh, I don't know. You might have me stumped."

Jeff's gleaming gaze jumped between Allison and Sara as they bantered back and forth. "I know," Jeff jumped into the fray. "You're the Little Mermaid!"

Sara giggled, and Allison joined in before saying, "You're clueless."

Will moved the pan off the heat. With his and Jeff's limited experience around children, he caught Jeff's gaze and grinned widely, clearly enjoying the silliness, too. "You can't be anyone other than Snow White." His contribution preceded a smoothly performed bow to both of his ladies.

The excitable child clapped her hands fast and loud. The shriek of glee let all the aching eardrums in the nearby vicinity know of her satisfaction. Sara reached out both hands, and Will immediately scooped her from Jeff's arms.

With the exchange completed, Jeff bowed to Allison. "If you would excuse me, Your Royal Highnesses." Jeff, with a nasally-sounding voice, took his role-playing quite seriously. Even as they joked, he couldn't help but imagine that some of it could be true. If nothing else, Sara looked like she had stepped out of a fairytale story of his youth. And Allison, well, she looked like a modern-day princess. "I will depart and let you partake in this morning's feast."

Sara had tucked her head shyly into her father's chest, and Allison's reaction couldn't be stopped. The picture of that adorable imp charming Will helped chip away some protective walls lodged around her heart and mind.

Shaking her head, getting back in the game seemed like a good distraction. Addressing Jeff in a proper comeback for this pretend exchange, she said, "Yes, of course, fine, sir." Allison held herself in regal stature. Emulating the Queen of England, she lifted her hand, graciously waving him farewell. "You are dismissed."

"As you wish, Milady." He clicked his heels in dismissal.

Her smile wobbled as Jeff swooped up the stack of pages on the nearby counter, tapped the edges against the hard surface, winked at Allison, and left the room whistling.

Oh, no. The warning popped into Allison's mind too late to do anything about it. She missed her chance to keep the discussion on Sara.

There went her distraction.

Chapter Four

Sara angled back in Will's arms, studying her father's face. Her usual devil-may-care expression was presently absent. Instead, a quietly determined look passed between father and daughter.

Allison stood frozen in place. With the two of them side by side, their likeness astounded her. More than Allison felt comfortable with.

Although, there were subtle differences between them too. Like Sara's eye color that got passed down from the Buchanan family tree. Plus, the shape of the eyes, the oval-shaped head, and the body type that took after Allison. There was no mistaking Will's skin and hair coloring, mouth and chin facial features. Not to mention the uncanny similarities to her father's mannerisms that helped Sara's paternal parentage stand out with their proximity.

Especially since Allison's new role interrupted the previous understanding of her role as Sara's aunt and surrogate mother. Allison's half-sister, Peggy and her husband, Bob, severed that masquerade the other night, and Will's legal proceeding made it official, putting an end to a three-year secret.

Sara would legally be Allison's daughter. The dark clouds hovering around the Buchanan's legacy would now affect Sara directly. Not to mention the complications that could arise listing William Maxwell as Sara's father.

Having special abilities came with dangerous conditions.

People like Will and Jeffrey Collins dealt with life-threatening situations all the time. This brought certain risks to them and the people around them, like their current investigation.

Allison shivered.

Will felt her fears projected into his mind and made another vow. However, not sharing this one with his bride didn't negate how binding he believed the vow to be. Will had no intentions of letting them go and would do everything in his power to wipe away Allison's doubts about their lives together.

Her childhood fear of a 'Buchanan family curse' needed debunking once and for all. Senator Buchanan held the answers, and Will was determined to expose the truth, too.

And that started with what got disclosed to Allison today.

Will's gaze was drawn toward his wife. A reaffirming purpose solidified like an unbreakable foundation.

They belonged together.

If pressing the issue and taking control of this situation rested solely on Will's shoulders, he would gladly carry the guilt.

Allison's hard-headedness didn't stand a chance.

"Ally, don't you see the resemblance to Snow White?" he prompted, then pushed a message telepathically. *Don't worry. Sara will be safe here.*

The magic trick with one small ball shuffled between three red cups held nothing on what lengths Will took after their ambush in Florida yesterday. Numerous flights had left their location and gone in multiple directions to hide this place.

Allison briefly hesitated before forcing her body to relax. It would serve no purpose projecting her fears onto her daughter. "I see the incredible likeness. I can't believe I didn't see it before. You look just like her, from the top of your dark hair down to the shiny black shoes."

"I know!" Sara giggled in delight and bounced happily in her father's arms. "I know. I look es... saclky like her. Can I be her? Can I be Snow White today?"

As Will held Sara close, a wave of emotions came crashing over him. Feelings so intense, he couldn't catch his breath. He had known this little girl for just one day, and already, he couldn't imagine his life without her. His jawline tightly clenched, as did his embrace around his daughter. But when Sara wiggled, he loosened his hold.

He bounced Sara playfully and watched her face light up, and her small chin angle upward–a look similar to her mother's. "Hey there, princess, you ready to eat a yummy omelet?"

"Yep! With ketchup," Sara excitedly added. Scrambling to get down, she dashed for the island where three place settings sat ready.

Allison quickly grabbed several pillows from the surrounding stools to stack on a counter-height, high-back seat next to the one on the end. She helped Sara up to that selected spot–that would provide a middle buffer.

But her plan got foiled when, after Will set the pan on the counter, he playfully gathered Sara and her pillows to plop her down one stool over. While his eyes glittered with humor, a stool got held out for Allison to take–right next to his.

A boom of laughter followed afterward when Allison stuck her tongue at him behind Sara's back.

****

The newly formed family finished breakfast in record time through animated conversation and mini-mishaps from Sara's independent eating habits. But all too soon, this pleasant reprieve came to an end.

Pressing matters were waiting for them.

Will turned to his daughter and kissed the top of her head. "Sir Jeff is looking forward to spoiling you. And you did a great job of eating all your breakfast. Do you want a treat?"

Does a fish need water?

Allison's reply got sent to Will.

"Chewbles!" Sara called out.

Will's head tilted to the side, clearly clueless on what this meant.

"She has chewable vitamins after breakfast and dinner," Allison explained. "I'll see if my sister packed them in with Sara's stuff." She also considered her daily regimen and added, "You didn't get my vitamins, too, by any chance?" With everything going on lately, she hadn't kept up with her daily routines.

"I didn't recall seeing anything in your medical cabinet," Will commented.

"They were in a drawer in the kitchen," she explained.

"No... sorry." Will distracted, spotting his daughter getting antsy, added without thinking, "How about a soda?"

"Yesss!" shouted Sara.

"Well, go find Jeff and get one," Will responded, clueless about what that sugar intake would do to his daughter.

"Just a small cup full," Allison corrected. Fully aware of the effects and not ashamed to use it to her advantage, she held up her hand, showing a small distance between the forefinger and thumb.

Will nodded and continued, "You two can hang out together for a little bit."

"Why?" Sara asked with a child's endless curiosity.

"Because your Mom and I just got married and want to spend time together talking about you." His finger playfully plopped down on his daughter's nose.

"Why?"

Allison's pressed lips, shaking shoulders, and sparkling eyes quickly conveyed that no help would come from that direction. "Because we need to decide where to go after my investigation," he explained.

This only resulted in Allison's smugness and Sara's stubborn expression. Will slowly set Sara on her feet. Following her down, he stooped to match her height.

He's a goner. Allison predicted as Sara pulled out the big guns.

Sara shyly communicated with sad eyes and pouty, trembling lips.

Will shot Allison a glaring pay-back promise before switching back to Sara. "Remember what we talked about this morning while getting dressed?"

Sara nodded her head up and down.

"Well, I need to talk to Mommy about it," he said.

Sara beamed up at him–like it was her birthday, and Will had just given her permission to open all the presents at once. Sara tilted her small head in thought, considering his request. "Just tell her I already knew you were my real Daddy."

His daughter's acceptance of their situation astonished him. He rained tiny, joyful kisses on her face.

Sara beamed at her father, then wiggled in his arms to face Allison. "Aun- Mommy, you better listen!"

"Alright, sweetheart." Allison leaned downward to press a kiss on her daughter's forehead.

"Do I get a kiss?" Will asked softly. A laugh followed when Allison stepped back and shook her head, expressing an adamant no.

But Sara disagreed, "Yes- You need to kiss Daddy too!"

Knowing her daughter wouldn't let this go, Allison groaned. Hastily leaning down again, resting her hands on Will's shoulder, she tried for a quick peck on the cheek.

Familiar with seizing any advantage, Will didn't let her get away with it. He reached behind with his free arm and tucked Allison closer to take control.

"Let go, Daddy." Sara squirmed to get out of the embrace. "I want a soda!" she shouted–already eager to move on to the next adventure.

Complying with the demand, Will slowly let his daughter go. Making sure Allison couldn't break free, he stood up, bringing his free arm around and successfully enveloping his new bride.

But Allison shifted around to see which direction Sara was headed.

"She'll be okay, Allison. The guard assigned to her went with her to the security room, and I sent a telepathic heads-up to Jeff."

With Will's mention of the guard, Allison stiffened. The relaxing atmosphere of the past hour had briefly obscured their present situation. And remaining strong during this forced reunion crumbled within mere moments of their time together.

She strengthened her resolve from here on out to do better.

Reading her like an open book, Will also strengthened his. Every figurative wall his wife erected to keep her protective shields he would knock down.

"Come on. Let's go upstairs." Will cupped her chin in his hand. "And I'll tell you the plan for the next few days. Explain to you the why's, the how's, and the if's. When there's a new development, I'll include you in the decision, too," he promised.

Allison tried stubbornly to pull from his hold, but Will didn't let go. He stayed equally firm in his objective. And he knew how to ensure all the barriers came between them.

And stayed down for good.

Chapter Five

In sensible low heels, Jennifer Daniels' footsteps were barely detected over the machine hummings, clashing of steel against steel, and the commotion of dockworkers coming and going. She glanced upward briefly. The stormy weather of the previous week had given way to sunny skies. Although a spring chill lingered in the late morning air, the weather report assured of rising temperatures as the day progressed.

But how often did they get that right?

She slowed her pace and casually turned her head, pointing her gaze in multiple directions. With her bland clothing and no-fuss appearance, she did well to blend into her surroundings at the Port of Wilmington.

A necessary skill for being very good at her job. And unlike the profession of a meteorologist, she couldn't afford to be wrong.

The importance of remaining unseen became her sole concern. When finding everyone too caught up in their own business to care about hers, she shot across the alleyway between two warehouses and eased against the age-battered door.

A small case got pulled from a large canvas bag tucked and secured on her left shoulder. After selecting the tiny metal picks needed, she got to work. Her movements were proficient, like always. Nothing too quick that may cause a mistake or cause undue attention, and nothing too slow that could mess with her well-organized timetable.

As the lock clicked open as expected, she applied light pressure, and the lever moved. The door slowly pushed inward. A cringe flashed across her face when the high-pitched squeaking sound proceeded with the hinges pivoting.

She held the door still and carefully made her way inside. Her skill made breaking and entering look effortless and not your usual expertise for an administrative assistant to acquire.

But Jennifer Daniels wasn't your standard office employee. And the 'whole world overthrowing organization' she worked for wasn't like most corporations.

More like the job to be avoided at all costs. But she didn't have the option of declining.

Plus, this morning's activities certainly could ante up the overall perception of how most people viewed her position in the organization. And if discovered, they would undoubtedly frown upon her current situation and have questions.

Her hand reached out to provide a tactile touch as her eyes

adjusted from the bright sunlight to navigating through the heavy darkness. The sounds from outside were muffled by the thick walls and limited glass windows on the facility's inland side. Any noises–from knocking items over or stumbling on the steps going up the metal staircase to the mezzanine level– carried easily. And not a preferred option if she could help it.

Upon reaching the upper landing, the passage shifted in direction. Once she opened the doorway into the corridor, a dim bubble of light shone ahead. Although no brighter than a large candle, this low illumination in the distance made her way inside much easier, and her pace quickened.

The call to meet was unexpected. So Jennifer didn't think anything good would come from this morning's get-together. Especially when all her reports lately came with bad news.

Mr. Black didn't like to hear the word 'no' or 'can't,' and she seemed to be putting those two unwanted words on rinse and repeat in most of their communications.

Her steps halted just outside the manager's warehouse office. The half-paneled glass door had become the source of the filtered light guiding her down the long hallway. As her hand reached out to take hold of the knob, the door swung inward.

Her chin jerked up, and her gaze locked with Black's trusted chauffeur, bodyguard, and overall confidant, Michael Arenald. The gun in his hand aiming in Jennifer's direction.

At first, they both froze in place.

Michael–who looked a decade or so older than Mr. Black–made the first move.

Stepping back, he motioned with his hand in a sweeping manner that Ms. Daniels couldn't ignore. When he continued to back further away, she straightened her slight frame, took that first step inside, and spotted who ordered today's meeting.

Mr. Black resembled his name to a 'T' with black hair, black shirt, and a black suit. Sitting before the cracked, linoleum-topped table, he looked so out of place with his pressed suit, classic silk tie, and impeccable grooming. "Ah... Jul-"

"Jennifer Daniels," she quickly corrected.

Mr. Black just nodded and continued, "Punctual as always." He gestured to the seat across from him. "Take a load off. Michael was kind enough to supply the latte and bear claw you prefer. God knows where you'd fit it all." He frowned as he studied her slim build still standing before him. "You've lost more weight," he rebuked.

Jennifer sat down with careful, controlled movements. The action had become so smooth and practiced that an average person wouldn't recognize signs of her training. But Black was hardly average and, like her–seeped so entirely in shadows–recognized a kindred spirit.

"Mr. Black, What is this meeting about?" she softly said as her direct gaze held his.

"We haven't met face to face in a while. I wanted to check in with you because Michael said he thought Sharpe was adding undue pressure-"

"Nothing I can't handle. Or you wouldn't have assigned this mission to me."

Mr. Black nodded slowly as his gaze continued to search her face and upper body. As if trying to find a particular cut or bruise upon her person. But he wouldn't find any.

Sharpe was cautious where he left his marks.

"I'm still convinced only you could get this difficult task completed," Black assured her. "Sharpe is ambitious, and his skill-set- Ahh... a necessary evil at this time. But if Sharpe's bad temper is bombarding you. Maybe something else could be-"

"Sir," Michael interrupted. "They are here."

When the proper, posh-sounding voice interrupted them, Jennifer spun around.

Michael's gaze stayed fixed on the built-in control desk along the opposite side of the room. One of the multiple screens showed movement within the dark shadows of the unloading conveyor belt and the loading division of the warehouse structure.

She turned back and studied Black's neutral expression, but he couldn't shield the flinty flash within his crystal-blue eyes. "You knew they were coming."

"Yes," Black replied. "Sharpe has been having me followed. I let it continue for a short time, but now matters being what they are- Well, I can't have eyes on us. And now I'll get several birds with one stone." Black's gaze remained on the monitor screens as the mercenaries spread out around the first-floor areas. "Sharpe is up to something."

His attention switched and fixed on Jennifer.

Called to action, she pulled several items from her large, sometimes cumbersome bag. Her hands moved in steady yet seemingly fluid motions, reflecting her practiced handling of weapons.

She halted when Mr. Black laid an open hand down on hers as she drew back the safety off her Sturm Ruger pistol.

"I need some of them alive, Ms. Daniels. They may have answers to our questions."

Jennifer nodded while readying her weapon and tucked it into her waistband. Her favorite throwing knife got inserted into the holder around her lower thigh. Her remaining semi-automatic gun settled in her right hand.

"Understood, Mr. Black." She slanted her stance toward Michael as he similarly prepared for engagement.

Of course, he had a lot more weapons at his disposal. Her

amazement at the amount–considering the heavy security protocols at the shipyard and not having her advantage– quickly passed to focus on their present situation. "I'm sure Michael and I can manage to maim most of them without too many fatalities."

She pushed away from the table and began to step back. Her movements becoming halted again when Mr. Black stood and raised his hand toward Michael.

As several weapons exchanged hands, Black automatically checked the bullet magazine and after finding it full, he used the palm of his hand to pull the slide stop to its rearmost position. This quick, two-beat, scrap-and-click sound released the gun to 'chamber-a-round,' making the weapon ready to fire.

He set the two guns down on the table, pointing them away toward an empty wall. Easing off his suit jacket, he carefully folded the costly garment along the back of a chair. His gaze went to Daniels' raised eyebrows before saying, "Ms. Daniels? Why should you and Michael have all the fun?"

Jennifer pressed her lips together and gave Michael–who had moved to the exit door–a pointed look. Their silent communication ended with Michael's slow nod sent back in kind. She glanced at the man most people wisely feared with frustration. "Don't get in our way, and everything should work out to your satisfaction." Jennifer's voice, although spoken softly, undoubtedly had that reprimanding tone as she followed Michael out.

Once passing the room's threshold she swung back to check on how her boss took the directive. Anyone–besides Michael and this wisp of a woman–wouldn't have believed what they were seeing.

An impish grin peeked out from Black's face before disappearing just as fast. "I wouldn't expect anything else," he admitted, moving behind her in an identical ready-stance fashion.

Chapter Six

Once Michael handed Jennifer and Mr. Black their earpiece devices, they all went in different directions. Their silent movements blended into their surroundings like ghosts passing through walls.

After reaching the lower level, Jennifer was the first to intercept one of their expected visitors. The singular clerestory structure along the entire length of the warehouse area provided enough illumination under the loading and unloading crane and tracking system.

Rookie mistake. She shook her head in mild reproach while spotting her prey darting among the post supports. She raised her weapon. With her aim focused on where less damage could occur–while still removing the threat–she fired her pistol.

Their first casualty fell to the ground.

She quickly eased around the stacked crates and tucked herself within their protection. After lowering her body mass to the ground, then pulling the unconscious man around to the side shrouded in darkness, she quickly disabled his weapon. Using his belt, she secured the first downed captive and whispered into her device, "One down, continuing to the east side."

Another gunshot went off into the vast space. Jennifer hesitated briefly before a soft voice spoke in her ear. "One down as well, Ms. Daniels. Care to wager a bet?" Jennifer shook her head over Black's cocky banter. "Yeah," she whispered back. "Losers cover a week's worth of laundry services for the winner."

"Ahh..." A slight pause proceeded before Black's voice continued, "You're on. Another one down." His voice came through with elevated breathing. "Keep in mind. Mine cost way more than yours to get dry-cleaned."

"Another down." Michael's refined dialect came through the earpiece as Jennifer came up beside a large piece of equipment. The dark brown, rusty pistons and wheel parts stood bigger than her person, not to mention the other metallic angled boxes and machine parts. She stayed close to the mechanical pieces. So oil and grime were most likely coating her white cotton shirt and gray pleated slacks as she moved alongside. "Oh. You'd be surprised how expensive my cleaning bill is each week," she joked under her breath.

Something ahead caught her attention when another silent migration–this time just a darker blur of obscurity–stayed concealed among the deeper cover of shadows. "I spy movement on the east, exterior facia. The mass size suggests possible three targets, maybe more."

"Stand down, Ms. Daniels. Let Michael and I handle this," Black's orders came through clearly, in a voice that meant business. But Jennifer chose to ignore it. Instead, she silently approached the warehouse section. Her path stayed close to the stacked crates adjacent to the warehouse's overhead doors on the Port's waterside. The large overhead crane provided ample coverage.

Massive metal posts stood side by side, approximately twenty feet between each. Their structural positions allowed the commercial transportation trucks to drive inside and unload the cargo before moving to the opposite overhead doors to exit the building.

She darted to the next pillar, pressed her chest tight to the metal plates, and peered around the post to track her prey.

Just as she was about to sprint to the next post in line, a large wooden crate hurtled through the air, heading in her direction. She had just enough time to jerk down to the floor before the box and its contents exploded into a shower of debris.

A large mass of rapidly-moving muscle engulfed her into a firm embrace, sending her heart racing faster than the flying objects had. A set of strong arms enveloped her, guiding her to safety behind a row of shipping containers as the barrage of projectiles continued.

"I said to stand down." Black's reprimand was whispered directly into Jennifer's ear as his mouth leveled close to her cheek. He set her down. As her feet touched the ground, she got spun around, and a frantic search of her person took place. He gently shook her when spotting no blood or bodily injuries on her person.

With breaths coming out in short puffs, he bent forward, resting each hand on his upper thighs.

Michael skimmed silently alongside them and pressed Jennifer Daniels behind him. When she tried to move around him, he blocked her. Turning toward the warehouse's entrance, he gestured, jerking his chin toward the three remaining figures, trying to pin them in on all sides.

The sun streamed through the high clerestory windows. The angles of bright light shone down on the group, highlighting their location. Their cocky movements into the open relayed their advantage as one of the men stood up ahead against the first set of posts.

His telekinetic power continued to shower debris in the vicinity where Jennifer and Mr. Black had stood just moments before. The two other men were carefully maneuvering around the broken containers and checking the opposite rows of shipping cargo that sat ready to be loaded and sent onward when business hours resumed.

Tucked safely behind Michael's back, Jennifer let out a soft huff. Her head shook from side to side at their over-the-top protectiveness. But then, the tall shipping container nearby gave her an idea. She tugged on Michael's shirt. "Hey, If you two help me, I can get a better view and lay down some cover."

Mr. Black turned around, saw Jenifer's hands resting on her hips, her chin cocked to the side, and met her challenged gaze. When glancing over at his top agent, bodyguard, and friend, he gave a grimace and a short sigh when Michael shrugged in agreement.

Jennifer quietly kicked off her shoes. The two men quickly lifted her, and she aptly climbed higher. As she got in place, Mr. Black and Michael went in different directions to loop around and come up behind their assailants. Jennifer shimmied to the edge of the container and stood ready to provide them some protection.

It didn't take long before she had a clear trajectory of the telekinetic individual spewing wreckage around them. With a press of her forefinger, she took her shot, and the target fell. Unfortunately, she couldn't take the chance of just maiming him due to his talent.

Her shot aimed to kill.

Some returning fire came back in her general vicinity. They

couldn't tell her exact location from her gun's singular report. Her next shots, however, would. So, she needed to make them count.

Coming around a corner, Mr. Black spotted his intended target. With his position set, he pushed the metal gear shifter to the ground. The metal hitting the concrete floor left a hollow-sounding 'ping' in the space around him. This got the attention of the man who was presently shooting at Jennifer.

The man swiftly shifted his bearing and directed a raised arm, holding the gun in Black's general direction.

Mr. Black held still and waited for the man to investigate. A few precious moments passed before the guy appeared at the edge of his peripheral vision. Kicking out his foot, Black removed the gun from the assailant's hand. The weapon clattered to the ground, and another wheelhouse kick followed through into his opponent's chest, sending the man crashing into the nearby debris.

The assailant recovered quickly, and his defensive moves of blocking hits and avoiding direct kicks soon got him in place to switch tactics. Black's attacker began flinging offensive strikes, and the two men sparred on equal footing. No sooner would one man launch into a series of forceful swings and kicks, did the other swiftly retaliate with equally aggressive moves.

Black charged again with another push, followed by a jab to the man's ribs. The receiver of those hits grunted before blocking further strikes to his abdominal area.

Suddenly, a heavy form emerged from the aisle way and tackled Black's assailant to the ground. Black stood ready but slightly winded. Michael jerked his chin up and leveled Black with a glaring look. "Sir. Stop playing," he grumbled and returned his attention to the man down.

As Michael subdued their captive and secured zip ties around wrists and ankles, Mr. Black stood unaware of the other man creeping close behind them. A gun in hand became lifted and the forefinger pressed on the trigger, aiming at Mr. Black's body.

A shot went off.

Mr. Black spun around just in time to see their last intruder fall.

"I think. That. Counts as a win, Mr. Black." Jennifer's sing-song voice spoken out-of-breath came over loud and clear through their ear devices.

Mr. Black turned toward Jennifer's hiding place only to discover she was not there. His hands came up to rest on either side of his hip. With a straining gaze he tried to locate her.

His eyes quickly widened when finding her new position. Figuring out that she must have jumped over two additional rows of shipping containers to make that shot, he shook his head and sighed heavily.

With restrained patience, he said, "Well, bloody shite. You get the win."

Chapter Seven

The holding cell was suddenly flooded with glaring, bright lights, dispelling the previous pitch-black darkness.

Robert Liston, the sole surviving prisoner from the Orlando Airport's altercation, blinked rapidly as the figures standing before him came into focus. His breathing quickly escalated as he jumped up from the reposed position on the singular cot in the small room. "I've told them nothing!" he pleaded in fear.

Edward Sharpe stood beside one of the rookie agents on guard duty at Maitland police department's small Federal Bureau's office. Sharpe's ungloved hand gripped the agent's exposed arm, and the conduit for his power remained fixed. His window of opportunity would never be better than this particular changing shift.

The young agent stood before the cornered prisoner, wearing a glassy-eyed, blank expression as the gun rose in his hand. And even as a shot got fired into the sound-proofed room, hitting its target at point-blank range, his demeanor never altered.

Sharpe's appearance, in comparison, held rigid features with a glint of cold fury reflected in his narrowing gaze. His hand remained firm on the young man as he whispered, "Good job, Special Agent Anthony. Now, I want you to escort me out, get in your car and drive away. You will go home, sleep, and not remember anything that happened here." He used his free hand to lower the arm holding the gun. "Put your weapon away first."

The newly appointed GS-5 agent eased his sidearm into the black FBI cant holster on his belt and snapped the fastener. The dead body and the blood pooling on the floor were ignored as the young agent led Edward Sharpe into the adjacent parking lot.

Sharpe turned in unison, keeping control of his tethered puppet. He exited through the door opening with one hand resting on the young agent's neck. "Stop," he said quietly, and the man immediately halted. Sharpe's free hand–wearing a dark-brown leather glove–pressed the toggle down and the room inside returned to darkness.

"Okay, Special Agent, lead on." Sharpe's smirk stayed in place the whole way through the nearly empty parking lot while lowering himself into the driver's seat. He received enormous satisfaction as Special Agent Anthony followed his powerful hypnotic suggestion, got in his white Honda Civic Hatchback, and drove away.

****

Will Maxwell had no idea the events conspiring against them would alleviate his present good mood.

Last night's actions and the report reviewed with Jeff over breakfast gave him reason to be confident. Plus, the decisions and plans made with Allison thus far pointed toward a promising future for him and his new family.

"Let me go check in with my team. I'll only be a few minutes. Then we can talk," he said, swinging his thumb upward and pointing to a nearby hallway that Jeff escaped to.

Allison jerked her chin in reply and stayed in place as her gaze followed him out. When he stepped inside a room down the hall, different from the one Jeff and her daughter got to, she tilted her head to the side.

She wanted to follow him, but, thought better of it. Instead, she pivoted around and headed for the main stairway. Figuring there would be plenty of time later to see what was happening with the investigation made her decision easy.

That is if Will stayed serious about sharing.

A guard standing discreetly near the front foyer had her pausing briefly before nodding and smiling at him. When the man acknowledged back, in the same manner, she said, "Good morning, I'm Allison… and you are?"

"Morning, Ma'am. Call me Pete."

"Oh, please call me Allison."

"No problem, Allison."

"Well, um. As you were." An awkward wave got sent back before she sat down at the stair's bottom landing, avoiding any further eye contact or conversation. Even after spending most of her life around security personnel, she still felt uncomfortable with the process.

Her body jolted when a sudden thought rose to the surface. If she remained married, this simple life she had enjoyed these past several years would be gone. Will's life was more than complicated. Adding in all the pomp and circumstances of the political sphere back in DC only further ensured that the old life she had given up with her uncle came back around with her connection to Will.

So would Sara's. Allison huffed and bolted up from the landing step.

Pete held in his grin as he watched his boss's new lady flirting around like a bumble bee from one flower to the next. Going up to the paintings on the walls to correct their leveling. Relocating accent pieces to different locations that looked fine where they were before. Plus, refolding blankets that he thought were already perfectly folded. To only end up back by the stairs, adjusting a sizeable ornamental mirror that was incapable of moving due to the fact they had screwed it in place when Will's property manager had it installed last week.

He figured Will had his work cut out for him and was never more thankful for his single status. Taking gunfire, in the young man's opinion, remained preferable over messing with a woman and their fickle nature any day of the week. If his experiences had taught him anything, a man should take things nice and easy. "The matters of the heart would only bog one down," he muttered.

Will came around the corner while Allison floated from one activity to the next. *Ahh, something got her going.* He determined while addressing Pete with a silent, hand-gesturing acknowledgment. He passed by the guard and moved up the stairs to stop at the middle landing.

Tilting her head up, Allison studied a wayward curl in the mirror's reflection as Will's image passed behind her.

Will noticed her delaying tactics and prodded her along. "You can't improve perfection." His chuckle held a hint of smugness.

Regardless of how often she pressed the misbehaving lock in place, it remained unruly. Allison snorted. "As if you-" Angling her head to make eye contact with him in the mirror's reflection, she lost her breath. Yet again.

Leaning down, resting on the banister, Will's forearms lay exposed. The tribal tattoo peaked out on his right-handed arm, his collared white business shirt pressed against his firm chest, and those well-worn jeans hugged his muscular thighs as he bent over. The pose was both casual and arrogant.

Catching the sound of her swift breath, Will's eyes darkened as he exchanged a quiet survey of his own. His slow, relaxed, devil-may-care grin made the pulse in her throat standout. "Like what you see, Ally?" he teased, one eyebrow rising in silent challenge.

"Oh, you're so full of it." Allison ran up the stairs and stopped three steps above Will's position. A fiery glint in her green eyes came close to leveling with a twinkling brown pair as he shifted around to face her. Their unspoken skirmish was still in play, and she added fuel to the fire.

"Come on… Ranger." Using her laughing eyes, sexy pose, and devious smile, she sought to leave him in ashes. "Your room or mine?" she said in a sultry manner. And with a quick tug on his ear, she ran up the stairs laughing.

Hearing that old nickname–playfully dubbed when they first met, and he had worked with the National Parks Services–he grinned. Encouraged and unable to lose a dare put him in motion. He nimbly moved up the steps to catch her.

Allison's quickening heartbeat went double-time when he scooped her up, threw her over his shoulder, and said, "Come on, slowpoke, we'll use ours."

"Show off," Allison yelled while hanging upside down, smacking his rear end.

He laughed, continuing up the staircase without breaking his stride. Another guard stood post at the front of the hallway as Will moved along. "Hey, Mike," he called out and kept going.

"Will," Mike responded, nodding to Allison while flashing a wide grin as she struggled to keep her view from turning topsy-turvy. "Ma'am," he said while their eyes briefly met before Allison gave up on remaining upright.

Juggling Allison's squirming body was pure torture. Her tempting curves were so easily accessible. He increased his speed and jogged to their bedroom. A lighthearted spank on Allison's rear end served as payment for maintaining his self-control before tossing her down on the king-size mattress. As he bounced on the bed beside her, he heard her squeal like a school-girl, and his mood lightened even more.

But that didn't last nearly long enough. From one moment to the next, the usual tension between them returned.

Tenfold.

In Will's experience, one never turned away any advantages–big or small, and this situation was no different. He eased physically away to give Allison some breathing room, but he refused to lose any metaphorical ground.

The traitor, Nancy Johnson, working for the Sons of Liberty, who put all this in motion, had gotten one thing right. Deliberately setting Allison up with Jake and Debbie's work-connection didn't occur on a whim. Keeping track of Allison's movements over the years– using his Guardians Inc.'s contract with Senator Buchanan–certainly gave anyone who was paying attention an idea of his intentions.

Hell... Will thought back to those times with his men, giving them a hard enough time with the constant need for more reports. *Above and beyond what I sent to her uncle.*

Even Will hadn't fully understood his motives at the time.

His grin skewed in a sinfully wicked manner. *I do now.*

Allison jolted when his wolfish expression stayed firm. Her fingers picked at the bedspread's raised embossed threading, trying to remain calm. But her gaze judged the distance to the nearest exit.

Will moved in quickly to kiss her cheek, causing Allison to jump two inches off the bed. Taking a calculated retreat didn't require heavy thinking. He bounced back just as fast and headed for the bathroom. "I've been getting some headaches," he admitted to her–all a part of his devious plan. "I'm going to have a soak in the whirlpool. It might help." He paused and swiveled back toward Allison, whose look of relief morphed into concern.

"I'm sorry," Allison said with a heavy sigh. "I don't want Sara and me adding-" She thought better of continuing that line of discussion and looked down at the comforter. She traced the floral pattern with her fingers.

"Allison, look at me," he softly commanded.

Dashing up from the bed led to further evasions rather than doing as he demanded. However, smoothing out the crease on the bed, adjusting the decorative pillows just so, and leveling the bedspread's bottom hem with the bedrails didn't take as nearly as long as she wanted. Her gaze darted around the room to find other similar busy work.

Her toiletry and other personal items on the dresser became her sole focus. She shifted toward Will and–with eyebrows raised high–finally met his gaze with a silent demand. Her personal items' appearance required an explanation.

"I had them moved in here with me. I put you in your old room last night, so it was familiar when you woke. I arranged for Sara to move into it when we were downstairs. It has a connecting door to this one."

"Oh," she replied, unable to formulate anything else. Even thinking about tonight's sleeping arrangements brought her heart rate up.

"You and Sara are the only good things to come out of this situation," Will continued to explain; knowing Allison so well made maneuvering his next steps easy.

She unconsciously moved her items in an aesthetically balanced manner, seemingly not listening to what Will said, but she took in every word.

"Allison-" Will stopped and took a deep breath.

With a tilt of her chin–that was all too familiar to Will–Allison swiftly faced him. "It should have been my decision. Us sharing a room."

Will didn't take the bait. Their sharing a bed was going to happen. It would be torture being so close and not touching her, but she needed to understand how serious he was about staying married to her. Instead, he pointed to the sitting area banking the bay windows.

Allison's gaze flew to the scattered files along the coffee table's surface.

"I brought some files up last night. And I will take you up on your offer to help. Jeff is going to keep Sara entertained for a couple of hours." He didn't miss the surprised glance she shot his way but chose not to respond. Not waiting for additional comments, he entered the bathroom, leaving the door ajar.

Grinning, he turned on the water and undressed. He was taking some advice heard long ago from an old family friend, Frank Marshall. At the time, Frank had been joking with Will's father and said, "When dealing with your lady love, walk a fine line between honesty and devilish sneakiness."

Will hadn't known what Frank had meant back then. But that sentiment became his guiding way today.

The steaming, pulsating whirlpool was at the perfect temperature when he fully submerged his body. He leaned back, sighed, and closed his eyes in satisfaction.

All the while, complaints of overbearing men and strong-armed tactics carried over the slamming of doors and banging of drawers.

As Allison loudly checked out her new accommodations, Will strategized his next move.

Chapter Eight

Supervisory Special Agent (GS-14) Matthew Culley placed the receiver of his phone down with a heavy thud. His eyes shut tightly, and a heavy sigh escaped him as he wearily tilted his head from side to side. Making that call was the last thing he wanted to do.

And it hadn't gone unnoticed that the person he had finished talking to hadn't appreciated the update either.

Like himself, the Associate Deputy Director, Frank Marshall, understood the significance of the latest news. All the leaks and lost leads within the multiple agencies had either turned up missing or, worse... dead. Leaving them with more unanswered questions. But something was becoming more and more evident by the hour.

They had several moles within their higher ranks.

The closed door of his office kept out most of the noise from the open office beyond. But he could still hear indistinct sounds from multiple conversations and the general office activity. Ringing phones needed answering, and the nearby copier dinged with a message that one of the trays was out of paper.

Culley drummed his fingers on the desk's surface while pondering the latest mystery. One that got added to all the other puzzles they had yet to figure out. Why would a rookie Special Agent stroll into the holding cell of one of their latest leads? Let alone shoot him dead.

The kid had had a promising future within the FBI until today's shocking events. No signs of insubordination or improper conduct in the past led up to today's shooting. He was the highest-scoring cadet in his graduating class last year. Mike Ragone in the IT Application and Data Division handpicked this new agent to work under him. All that remained to wait was to complete this brief assignment within Maitland's field office.

And pondering the strangest thing of all, his head shook in frustration. Young, Special Agent Thomas Anthony, son of Judge Thomas Anthony, Sr.–of Florida's Judicial District Court– had no recollection at all that he committed this cold-blooded murder.

****

Allison finished reviewing the last file, slamming it down on the table's surface. She stood up and headed toward the bathroom with swinging arms and stomping feet after more than an hour had passed. "If he thinks ignoring me is the way to go, he has another thing coming," she muttered.

Pushing the door fully open and storming inside, she came to a screeching halt.

The bathroom, hazy with steam, still revealed her miscalculation. The whirlpool tub upstaged the large room, and the pulsating jets caused thousands of tiny bubbles. However, those bubbles did not obscure the view of the man reclining in the tub.

She became transfixed by the sight of all those delicious muscles.

With eyes slightly closed, it hadn't been difficult witnessing her abrupt entrance with all the noise she made with her approach. The tub's jets created a soothing white noise and drowned out Will's slow exhale. His eyes fully opened as Allison remained frozen, unaware of his gaze. Will cleared his throat.

Allison jumped. "I, I-" she stuttered, whirling away, giving him her back. "I wanted to know if you were okay. I can see that you are so... umm. I'll leave you to-."

"Did you read the files?" Will asked, delaying her departure.

She paused. "Yes, I finished."

"Good. You can stay, and we can go over them."

"No! I don't think that's a good idea." Allison replied, gripping the door lever nervously. Understanding Sanctuary stood just a few steps away.

"I guess you're right." Will grinned before adding, "I'll need the files in front of me."

Allison let out a sigh of relief. Escaping this misstep was

moments away.

"But first, can I get your help with washing my back? My head is still pounding."

She shook her head in opposition.

Calculatingly, he pushed on, "Please... I promise to behave."

"Oh..." Shoulders slumping in defeat, she slowly exhaled. Spotting a pile of bath linens had her grabbing a bath towel. "Here." She dropped the towel in the water. "Put that around you."

"It's not like you haven't seen me naked before," Will dryly commented.

"Just do it," she commanded.

He adjusted the towel on the water's surface before leaning forward to get a washcloth.

Allison reached for the soap, but she pulled back when it brought her too close for comfort to an appendage of his that remained obvious even under the towel. "Can you hand me the soap, too?" she asked.

He turned slightly away before shooting her a quick smirk. Handing, her the washcloth and soap, he joked, "I will behave myself, I assure you."

Stalling, trying to prepare herself to touch his warm, smooth skin and the hard contours of his back, she took the time to lather up the soap. Just do it. She urged herself on before taking the cloth in her hand and, without looking, began to scrub.

"Whoa- Allison, leave some skin." Will winced and pulled away slightly.

She glowered in frustration. Shaking her head–not quite sure how she got herself in this situation–she made her motions slower and lighter.

"What did you think of the candidates we picked to watch, Sara?" Will asked.

"Umm," she said, unable to organize her thoughts. The closeness and feeling of his muscular back–even with the washcloth providing a buffer–caused quite a distraction.

Will, aware of her discomfort and shamelessly taking advantage casually commented, "I'm leaning toward the Patterson woman. Her brother, a consultant and friend, gave a glowing review. Since Sean rarely gives anyone such high praise except his wife and child, it holds some consideration."

Allison's chin tilted upward. "Why? She seems new to the division. Plus, I didn't see anything that led me to believe she has experience with children." Warming to the topic, she leaned down, and half sat on the edge of the glass-tiled ledge.

"I know, but I worked with her on a minor assignment before and liked her thoroughness. Ahh..." When Allison moved to a particular area near his shoulder, a grunt of relief escaped when the tight muscles loosened.

"Hmm," Allison focused more on that spot. Discarding the washcloth, she used her hands to massage him. "You're tight here."

Will sat up and bent forward, giving her more access to his back. "Plus- Ahh, that feels great. Sean has an infant, and the rest of his siblings have children. From what I could tell, she's around them a lot and loves it. She'd even started adoption papers on a little girl in Indonesia."

Committed to the task, wanting to give him some relief from his throbbing headache became her sole goal. Allison let her thoughts wander away from the investigation and kept silent.

Giving up on having a conversation, Will relaxed, letting his chin fall to his chest. That driving need, pushing him to keep all the balls in the air, eased into contentment. The sound of water pulsating and Will's grunts and sighs soon filled the space.

Breathing heavily with exertion, she enjoyed feeling the hardness of his well-fit body slippery with soap. A palm skimmed the circular tattoo that sat off-center on his shoulder and weaved into the tribal artwork that ran down his right arm. Her massage traveled to the lower regions, pressing into his hips and lower back contours.

Having Will succumb to her touch gave her a sense of power.

It held its own seduction.

The room's warm temperature, the bathwater, and the percolating of the air jets made the space feel like a tropical oasis. Having this slice of time, with no fighting or tension, gave them a bit of normalcy. A reminder of what they could have if and when peace became possible.

They both took advantage of this and encouraged the quietness.

Until the water began to cool.

And unfortunately fell in sync with Will's drive to press forward. The upcoming battles snagged his focus away from this slice of heaven. Both his country's enemy and Allison's emotional barriers required vanquishing. Will eased away from her hands. "I better get out before I go back to sleep."

Allison's eyelids slowly blinked before she answered, "Okay." Gesturing with awkwardly formed hand signals indicated an immediate departure. She wanted to escape this delicately weaved intimacy.

Will's slight hold of Allison's arm stopped her. "Don't go," he quietly urged. "Why don't you hand me my robe while I dry off?"

"Okay," she whispered. Becoming mad at her inability to break away from his nearness when her thoughts screamed to do so. She quickly made her move to his thick, cotton robe resting on a nearby hook. She whirled away, giving him time to step out and dry himself. As she angled back, holding the ends of the robe open, he quickly wrapped the towel around his hips.

Guiding one arm in the sleeve, he released the towel to put the other arm through. He belted the robe, rotated again to face her, and slowly stepped forward.

"Why are you not angry with me about Sara anymore?" Allison's barely-there voice cried out. Remembering yesterday, the vibrating anger radiated off him before and during their wedding.

"Because. I understand why you thought you had to do what you did," Will answered, coming closer. He knew what drove her.

Fear.

Allison longed to belong, but she kept herself separate from those she cared about. Deciding it was safer made this action necessary. Or so she thought. He didn't understand that when they first parted ways. However, the many photos studied over the years gave him a better insight into what made her tick.

Her face, caught in numerous yearning expressions, came through loud and clear in many of those reports landing across his desk. They had tugged on his heartstrings and brought many troubling dreams at night.

She shook her head back and forth, hands held before her, pleading with him to stay away even as her eyes said something else. Something she didn't even understand herself.

But Will did.

Careful not to startle her, his arms enfolded her. He lightly kissed her lips.

Allison yielded to his touch. Whatever magic spell formed around them during this peaceful interlude remained powerful. Her muscles stayed loose like she had been the one who had the massage. She floated away on the dream-like sensations as a pair of hands moved up her body slowly. Allison's arms hung relaxed by her side. She leaned in, sighing when Will gently cupped her face.

His embrace did not show force but held her to him in an unbreakable spell. The kiss felt like being drugged, an unmooring from her physical self that allowed her spirit to float away and glide on a wave of pleasure. Just pleasure.

She had to put effort into raising her arms and linking them around his neck. Her fingers brushed through his locks, damp from the steam of his bath. She reveled in the texture of soft volume, silky threads, and the curved contours of his neck and shoulders. All while their lips took turns sampling each other's taste. She became lost in the richness of flavors.

He molded her softness closer. Pressing hands, wanting to revisit all the swells and dips of her body, became a wonderland of tangible explorations. He would never get enough of her. The need to lay her down and peel away the barrier shielding her from him, like opening a present, overwhelmed him.

Them, skin to skin, was one hell of an incredible gift to

resist.

But the ringing of a nearby phone interrupted them. Will halted.

His fingers dug into her waist. Becoming aware of his surroundings again, he slowly eased back to study Allison's face.

She kept her head tilted back, eyes closed, while gently cupping his face with her hands. He relied heavily on the slivered amount of control left of his body's reaction to their closeness. "That's probably Jeff," Will softly explained, trembling, reining in his inner struggle. He forced his hands to fall away.

Allison slowly raised her eyelids and met his stare. Her witch's eyes were now more gray than green, and Will saw desire in their smoky depths.

"Thank you, Ally. My headache is completely gone." His voice sounded as if the words struggled to escape pass his throat and lips. And thankfully, the persistent ringing of the phone prevented any further communication between them.

Not knowing if this interruption was a nuisance or a Godsend, he broke away to pick it up and swiped across the screen to accept the call. "Yeah, what's up?" He paused to listen. "Hmm, that's right. I did." He nodded. "Okay. We'll meet down there."

His forced chuckle proceeded Allison's, and his eyes met in

the mirror's reflection over by the counter. "No- She'll probably have lots to say on that topic. But let's look into purchasing a commercial building in town." Another chuckle followed, more lighthearted than the first. "Don't call my daughter an Ankle Buster, bro. Yeah, you do that. Mike has some experience with children." Pressing the disconnect button on his cell phone, he ended the call.

"He's expecting us to be down in a few minutes." Will's expression and body language stayed seemingly unburdened, but his thoughts were anything but.

When Allison remained quiet, Will tugged on the robe's belt. His head tilted toward the door. "Come on, Ally. Let's get this meeting over with before your uncle gets here."

Following a slight pause, she swept her arm in a wide arc toward the door and said, "After you."

He headed to Allison but stopped.

Should I tell her about Guardians, Inc. being hired by her uncle?

His mouth opened to speak but then closed. His head shook from side to side. Bending down instead, he picked up the tossed towel, sloppily folded it, and placed it on the edge of the tub. The bath water began to recede when he released the stop. After snagging the wet towel, he rang it out and put it on the one he folded.

All the while, Allison kept silent, watching and wondering.

What was he going to say?

The clothes he wore into the bathroom sat on the floor by the tub. Will reached down and snatched them up. Before easing them into the nearby laundry basket, he searched his front pocket and pulled out a gold coin.

The coin had been given to him as a child by his grandfather. And Will took it everywhere with him. He even made the odd image on one side of the coin, his company's logo. His finger traced the edges of the design, a floating eye above a pyramid.

Fingering the embossed surface, he stood before Allison, promptly kissed her forehead, and left her alone in the hazy and humid bathroom.

Chapter Nine

J effrey Collins, fully immersed as Special Agent in Charge (GS-14) with FBI's Counterintelligence Division, was on the phone when Allison and Will walked inside the library. Of course, Jeff–doing what he usually did–half leaned, and half sat on the edge of the desk, resulting in Will gesturing for Allison to take the nearest seat closest to his partner.

Purposely bumping against Jeff's side and heading toward the desk, Will sat at the chair near his laptop across from Allison.

Jeff gestured with his middle finger while moving to the chair beside Allison. He pulled the phone line across the desk closer to him.

"Yeah, understood. He just came in, Sir." Pushing a button on the phone, he cradled the receiver between his chin and shoulder. "It's the home office. The report from Robert Liston's interrogation is missing, and he showed up dead. The same thing happened to Agent Thompson."

One of Jeff's many duties within the FBI, and the most natural choice due to his close friendship with Will, had him standing as the liaison between his agency and Guardians Inc.

"Not surprised. After he allowed Nancy to escape, Thompson was no longer useful," Will said. "Our enemy doesn't like leaving a trail."

Jeff nodded in agreement and then tilted his chin toward the phone. "They want to go over the information you found." Most knew Will as the information research specialist but didn't quite know how he gathered it.

Allison stood to leave.

"No, stay. I want you in on this." Will locked eyes with Jeff. "She can't go anywhere until this all plays out, making her a part of all this. She's officially on my company's payroll. Any problems with that?"

"Hell no. From what I have seen so far, she thinks fast on her feet." He sent her a grin. Seemingly showing no hard feelings from yesterday when Allison tricked him, took his wallet full of cash, and left what little of his pride remaining to escape to Florida.

"We can certainly use more help, and it's a plus that it's someone we trust." Having said his piece, Jeff spun back to the phone and reconnected the call. "We're all here," he announced to their caller before adding, "Will brought an associate with his company on board. Supervisory Special Agent Matthew Culley, say hello to Allison Maxwell." Jeff grinned when catching Allison's startled expression from hearing her new last name for the first time.

"Will," the caller replied and then wearily sighed. "If you say she's good, that's all I need to know. We have a situation. Deputy Director Frank Marshall said this needs your immediate attention."

To be among a limited group having special abilities in the world's population who didn't could lead to the spreading of worldwide panic. Or worse, subjugation of their kind. So, only a few within the agency knew about individuals like Jeff and Will.

Frank Marshall was one of those few men.

"Okay, Matt, let's break it down." Will smiled while looking at Allison, then got down to business.

"We lost the crucial lead in the case..."

Allison sat quietly and listened as the caller described a series of disjointed events that required a link. Grabbing a notebook nearby–for her, it helped to write things down–she started taking notes as the conversation flowed around her.

Unfamiliar with the agency's protocol, one central question stood out in her mind. *Is it unusual to be so easily included?* Either they were incompetent fools who let anyone in on an investigation as serious as this, or Will had a lot of pull.

The call still proceeded well over an hour later. Allison's notes spread over nine pages so far and her hand began to cramp. Will worked on his laptop, concentrating on the caller and pulling up research while talking.

Allison did not think men could multitask well, but the proof sat before her, dispelling that misconception. And she liked seeing Will this way: like getting to peek behind the curtain to see the Great and Powerful, OZ.

Flipping to a blank page, she caught Jeff's concerned look when she shook out her writing hand again. She shot him a quick wink back before bending over her notebook and continuing to write.

Soon afterward, the Supervising Agent began wrapping up the call, dividing responsibilities and resources across numerous divisions, other intelligent agencies within our government, and Will's company. Jeff disconnected the call, ending the meeting, and Allison could finally look up past her notebook pages.

Will, typing, paused to position his mouse accordingly. Clicking numerous times, then resuming his typing, he gestured for Jeff to hold on a moment. A few more clicks on his mouse had a nearby printer spewing pages. Absently combing through his hair, pushing strands away from his face, he swiveled to retrieve the printed sheets to face his audience.

Jeff chuckled at Allison's expression—who gave a good

imitation of an owl with wide, blinking eyes. "Yeah… that's why we put up with his shit. He is a walking CPU with high output processing capabilities. Or what I like to call the mystical bad-ass master that allows us all to skate through the backdoor tube of global information.

"And that's without him using the woo-woo abilities," Jeff said, pushing off the desk and stretching out his arms. With everything from his sea-blue colored eyes, dirty-blonde hair worn loosely around his face, bold-print, button-down, collared shirt, and ripped jeans, he looked more at home on a beach than inside an office.

Unaware of Allison's scrutiny–or, more like, unconcerned– Jeff continued, "Believe me. You don't want to see that strange shit if you don't have to. His eyes-" Jeff raised his hands to his face to showcase around the eyes. He rolled the eyes back into their sockets and mainly showed the white portion of his eyeballs.

Will's face turned flush. "Quit it, Jeff."

"I'm not sure what that all means," Allison admitted. "But, I agree with his output capabilities."

This time, Allison's face blushed pink with embarrassment when both men turned to look at her with their mouths held open. "No! God, no, I meant the computer. Output with the computer." Allison's laugh was self-deprecating. "Can we stay on task? Get your minds out of the gutter."

Jeff shrugged. "We're guys. We practically live there."

"Okay." Grinning, Will brought the pages around the front of the desk, spreading them out for them all to see. "This here-" He pointed to several articles. "Is everything I could find about the Copperheads, formed during the Civil War.

"They were Confederate sympathizers located beyond the Union lines. The largest group was called the Knights of the Golden Circle. Later known as the Order of The Sons of Liberty. I think they're just calling themselves Sons of Liberty."

"Why all the Civil War references?" Allison asked. "I know the South can be a little touchy sometimes with Yankees, but we're a big melting pot at this point.

"Most of my mother's family came from the South and still reside there. But I and a handful of distant cousins live up North. Besides some friendly ribbing about the Yankee way rubbing off on us when I visit, I'm not sensing any deep hatred."

"I'm not sure if it's specifically about the South's outcome in the war," Will explained while straightening the papers on the desk. "Or the possibility of going through another one. There is a dark web room labeling it as a 'Revolution in Evolution'."

"Catchy. But what does it mean?" Allison asked as she slowly rotated her head, easing the tightness around her neck muscles. She tilted her head to the side and gave Will a slight frown.

"Good questions," Will replied. "From what I could gather from my cyber-sweeps and what our inside mole could determine, they obviously have a different political agenda."

The term cyber-sweep, labeled by Jeff a few years ago, was a good enough description of Will's unique ability than anything else. Now, everyone involved with the investigation used the same term. But not all were aware of the exceptional gift Will possessed. Like most, they assumed his computer hacking skills got him noticed by the agencies' higher-ups.

"But we're not sure what that looks like right now. I think dictatorship is their end goal, but they'll put a pretty spin on it to get public support. Nancy Johnson mentioned Andrew McKnight to me," Will said as his fingers drummed on the desk's surface.

That unnerving call felt like it happened weeks ago instead of a few days ago.

"Yeah, the novelist. What about him?" Jeff leaned on the

desk and filtered through some of the pages. That quick conversation between Nancy and Will had brought up much more than Andrew McKnight.

Jeff had been the one to file the report of that call's transcripts to the home office when Will failed to do so. Jeff's sixth sense came to an immediate surface with the mention of the author. He just knew it meant something important.

But what could it be?

Chapter Ten

Snatching up a file from the floor, Will threw it on top of the pile and pointed to a close-up of the author with a caption about his new book. "Andrew McKnight specializes in political concepts, the history of governments, political societies, and world history."

"Are they looking to get ideas from him? Pick his brain on strategies?" Jeff asked.

"I think they're way past strategies. They've been moving and implementing their plan into action for years. Each move is calculated and determined to a precise conclusion. They don't need Andrew for ideas," Will remarked.

"For public support," Allison whispered.

"Exactly." Will pointed his forefinger toward her and then poked at the author's picture. "They will want him to write a book. They probably feed into public fears about what's happening worldwide and then sell them on the Sons of Liberty's movement.

"They're fighting this war with backroom deals and propaganda. But I'm betting they'll follow up with a war if they have to. They'll have assassinations planned for key political figures. They probably already took care of some lesser noticeable figures in some fashion. Ones that couldn't be persuaded or controlled by their usual methods."

"Andrew's books are bestsellers," Jeff added, viewing the information through the web browser on his cell phone. "He's a frequent guest host for multiple political radio, cable shows, and blog casts. McKnight reaches both sexes because he talks politics, and middle-aged housewives think he's hot–" He looked up and gave Allison a grin when hearing her chuckle. "And no, I'm not speaking for me. Will's administrative assistant thinks he's Rad."

Jeff pushed off and began to pace. "God, Will. McKnight could do it! He'd have a clean-wave." He stopped and pivoted to face the other occupants in the room. "I wouldn't be surprised if he possesses a charismatic talent or something."

Coming closer to the desk, Jeff snagged the report. "He's been missing for several weeks now."

Jeff leafed through the file. "His publisher received an email right after McKnight went missing, citing some shit about needing to clear his head to get ideas moving for a new book.

But get this: McKnight's son, Tommy, is four and a half years old, and he went missing from his daycare a few days before Andrew.

"And then the daycare got a call from Andrew hours later, claiming it was a family mix-up, and his son was back home. He followed up by canceling the childcare services for a live-in nanny agency instead. When the daycare director explained that they needed something in writing due to school policies, one was sent shortly afterward. No one has heard from either one since.

"Oh- and the letter to the daycare-" Jeff smacked the sheet of paper and added, "Had a penny in the envelope. The daycare director didn't know what to make of it. We had both items tested for other prints and trace evidence; nothing showed up."

"What's the significance of the penny?" Allison asked.

Will explained, "A copper penny got left at different sites for the Copperheads during the Civil War when they wanted to claim responsibility for an attack or distraction."

"Like a terrorist calling card," Allison assumed.

"You could say that," Will said, reaching his fingers into his front pocket to touch his gold coin. Pulling it out, he tumbled it between his fingers. This movement–more like a muscle

memory at this point than any other conscious decision–
always helped him to think.

"In the past, as political opportunists, they took credit for
mishaps or unplanned riots when convenient to their cause.

"Unfortunately, today's namesake is a lot more directly
active. They don't mind getting their hands dirty as attack dogs
for the parent group. These were the thugs Nancy sent out for
you." Will met Allison's gaze and looked away. Letting go of his
coin to scatter other reports on top of the desk, he continued,
"But get this. He's not the only one taken."

They were close to finding a connection. Allison could feel it
in her bones. Will paused briefly to lay out sheet after sheet of
photographs with articles on the desk, like a winning hand at a
poker game.

"I searched for others when Andrew's name came up in the
investigation. Several high-ranking political figureheads went
missing only to show up back in their offices several days later.
At least six Fortune 500 companies ranging from marketing to
real estate have had their owners or CEOs disappear.

"All had rather poor explanations: taking a leave of absence,
extended vacations, and starting up new satellite offices, for
explaining their disappearances. No one is investigating
because there is no proof of any wrongdoing, and the

occurrences got scattered across a wide geographic field."

"But what can they want with businessmen?" Allison asked.

"Maybe the type of business? Marketing, real estate, government-supported business, and media," he listed out while shuffling through the information. Looking up from the papers, he asked, "What is the connection?"

"What about security companies, specifically computer networking software?" Allison shifted through some files she had been reviewing during their call. Will's comment had sparked a realization about a specific reference she circled in her notes. She flipped to that place and found the corresponding source in the file.

Will shook his head no, leafing through his notes. "Nothing yet, no companies relating to security, but there is one with networking. Why? Did you come across something?"

"Nancy said something about you visiting." Allison was re-reading the message. "Yes, here it is; Nancy said. I need to get everything set up first for your visit. Then she mentioned a secure location, yadda yadda, okay, here it is: 'You know security is the most important, don't you? I mean, you live and breathe it. Right, Will?'"

He shot a look toward his partner. When Jeff just shrugged,

Will turned his gaze back on Allison. "Okay, what's that got to do with anything now, Ally?"

"Okay, first, don't call me that. You know I hate it. Second, hear me out. Here's the last bit of dialogue, and I think it's the answer: 'To make sure Allison is dead. It's the most important thing.' That's it! Will. You're what she wants!"

"Yeah, she's an obsessive narcissistic individual who wants what she can't have- at your expense!" Will moved to Allison, pulling her into his arms. He ran his hands up and down her back.

Allison pulled away excitedly. "Listen, Will. It's not about me at all! It's always been about you."

Jeff reeled around, facing Allison. The puzzle piece clicked into place. "Oh rocker, Ally-" When spotting her fiery glare, Jeff hastily added, "Sorry, Allison. That's it!"

"Would someone tell me what the hell is going on?" Will demanded.

"He doesn't see it." Allison frowned and looked at Jeff.

"I know." Jeff looked at Will. "He's too close. Any mention of you and he gets worked."

Will spun around to Allison and gently shook her. "Just tell me!" Allison nodded, pushing him gently back onto the desk.

He sat down, waiting.

"The organization wants you. Nancy was just a tool to get to you."

Will opened his mouth to argue, and Allison gently put her finger on his lips to add, "First, you own one of the biggest security software companies in the country. Second, you design security systems and programs for private and government-supported agencies. Third, you have a contract with the FBI and other government security departments.

"And lastly and most importantly, they must know about your talent for interfacing with anything electronic, especially computerized. Will, you are the biggest backdoor into their opposition's operation they could find!"

Allison and Jeff watched Will as the pieces fell into place.

"You were the decoy." Will blew out a short burst of air when spotting Allison nod in agreement. He stood up to pace back and forth in front of Jeff and Allison. "I was sunk deep into no-man's land working. My parents were too risky to snag; taking them could risk exposure. My father is an ex-senator with significant security measures from the Secret Service and my company's men. Plus, the high-security programs I set up for them.

"They couldn't get to Jeff because he stuck close to my side. And of course, I've distanced myself from many others over the last few years because of this investigation. So, that left-"

Will stopped. His gaze zeroed in on the beautiful woman before him. His obsessive interest, disguised as security protection on Allison over the years, didn't fool anyone except himself. And Nancy most certainly caught on to that fact right away.

His pacing started again in an agitated manner. "That bitch played me."

Allison snagged him at his next loop around, catching his hand. "Even the smartest man on earth is still dumb regarding his lady." Allison brought him closer, pulling him down so she could land a soft kiss on his lips. "You really did have feelings for me all this time."

Will eased forward, leaning his forehead on hers, and said, "Yeah... and it only took a conniving bitch who threatens you–so she can kidnap me–to help me see it."

"Tubular, lovebirds, now that we see a bigger piece of this puzzle, let's take-off. Knowing the reason for Nancy's baiting can be used to our advantage. This may help us find out what they will do next and lay a trap to catch these bastards."

"Where are we going?" Allison picked up her notebook, closed it, and pivoted to leave.

Will snagged her arm and shook his head from side to side. "Nowhere. Take-off is to catch a wave. Hang around him long enough; you'll begin to catch on. Well... mostly."

"Oh." Allison grinned at Jeff, then pulled away from Will. "Now that I cracked this case wide open, I'm going to excuse myself and let you two do your thing. Sara is probably antsy by now. Be ready to take a food break-" She looked at her watch and added, "in about an hour or so. Can I call in here on an extension number?"

"Yeah. Just push Astrix–zero–four on the phone, and it will buzz in here." Will swung her around, dipped her low, and laid an enthusiastic kiss in appreciation. "I should have brought you onboard a long time ago."

"Yes-" The excitement waned in Allison's face with the influx of worry. "No- Oh, no, Will. Don't you see?" The loss of so many others from mysterious attacks in her life caused a ripping fear in her heart. Spurring her on, she cried, "You need to get far, far away from us. Go back to where you stayed buried and out of their reach in DC." Allison grabbed her notebook and stormed out.

Will stood shocked. His attention centered on the door that

slammed closed. "Just great. The Buchanan curse again. She found yet another excuse to put distance between us."

Jeff came around and stood facing him. "Will, she may have a point."

Chapter Eleven

Allison kicked the bedroom door closed, and a loud bang resonated through the upper level.

The force with which she slammed the door only managed to alleviate a small fraction of her frustrations. Needing to reevaluate her relationship with her husband caused her to fume and fret about getting too close and losing focus on the big picture.

An embroidered pillow lying innocently on the bed was a victim of numerous punches before she plopped down without her usual gracefulness, sinking back against the bedding and staring upward. She sighed heavily and studied the moldings adorning the high ceiling while thinking about her current predicament.

Two days had passed since the break in the case. During this time, Will and Jeff had theorized that until they could determine a course of action with this new information–one that best targeted the terrorist organization–their present arrangement would be the safest route for all of them.

She still wasn't entirely on board with him remaining here. Not only for his safety but finding out that her feelings toward Will hadn't been one-sided only made her situation even more difficult. His nearness brought challenges and pushing him away wasn't as easy as it had been before.

Will is the most stubborn, know-it-all man I have ever had the misfortune to...

Allison's head shook repeatedly, dispelling the rest of that thought. She reminded herself it would be better to focus on other things.

"Guardians Inc. did postpone the visit with my uncle," she said, stroking the surface of the bedspread like she was making a snow angel with her arms. Her brightly colored poolside cover-up stood out against the subdued off-white textures of the bedding ensemble.

After that momentous meeting that shifted the case dramatically, a short phone call to her uncle worked to their advantage. Of course, this decision had incited Senator Buchanan's wrath, who demanded that Allison and Sara return to his family's estate.

Just as persistent, Will had notified her uncle of their

marriage and his rights as a husband to Allison and a father to Sara. He also stated that this allowed additional protective jurisdiction within the federal agencies and his security firm.

Allison stood up and paced alongside the foot of the bed into the lounging area and back. She feared Senator Buchanan would find a way to prevail with his government connections. "But Will already took steps to keep our whereabouts unknown," she reassured. Saying the words out loud gave them more weight. "And he did move fast where Sara was concerned."

Scheduled interviews for their daughter's personal care and protection had been quickly organized. Will had stressed to Allison and Jeff that they wouldn't go any further on the compiled list if they found one suitable agent.

With pull from Will's family friend and high-ranking player, Frank Marshall, they had selected Agent Rebecca Patterson.

Jeff had been insistent that two other agents become scheduled backups. Allison's suspicion of his not wanting their first choice became confirmed after Agent Patterson's meeting. Although he agreed with their logical choice, his head shook, and he mumbled something before abruptly leaving the library.

Allison also picked up on their newest team member's

response. Seemingly wary on screen, Rebecca's gaze had followed Jeff's quick departure from the video camera's view before it jerked back to Will and Allison.

"But Jeff and Will didn't disclose anything more other than citing a personal disagreement in the past." She mused out loud, recalling that the conferencing video didn't diminish the vibes that radiated between those two. Closer proximity was sure to be even more intense. She continued to pace around in the room while muttering complaints about being kept in the dark about a lot of things. "Shouldn't I know all the details concerning my daughter's protection?" she asked, looking around the room in frustration.

Because past experiences had taught her well.

The fears regarding her uncle had always proved spot on in the past.

Frank Marshall told Will that Senator Buchanan was pulling some strings and getting orders sent for Jeff's team to keep him apprised of the situation. By general concession, everyone understood the more decisions made in the next days, the more they could evade disclosing when those orders became official.

Another heavy sigh escaped Allison's lips. The faint sound got absorbed in the surrounding space. The tranquil interior of her luxurious bedroom continued to be overlooked. Her mind struggled in opposing directions on many personal fronts, and restless nights worked against her.

And when sleep did come, her nightly visits from her uncle made things even more confusing. "It has to be wishful thinking on my part," she whispered, remembering him urging her to work closely with Will, which completely contradicted with what she had experienced in the past or their recent communications. "They appear to be two different people."

And ever since that video-conference meeting with Rebecca Patterson, nothing else made sense.

She began questioning her sanity, especially with Will.

His behavior, more than all the rest, played on her uncertainty. Instead of directing all of his time to resolve this threat–a danger explicitly targeting him and, in turn, them– Will acted as if they were taking a holiday together.

Her direction of movement brought her near the bed. She flopped down on the mattress and splayed length-wise across it. "We are not on vacation!" Allison shouted into the nearest pillow, finding Will's presently loving, reasonable, and supportive demeanor impossible to handle.

"And I don't want Sara and my personal belongings packed

up and shipped to a safe storage location, like his parent's house," Allison complained under her breath, not ready to make changes once this investigation was behind them.

According to Will, it became the next logical step to take.

"Not for Sara!" She twisted around on the pillows and stared mindlessly at the ceiling again. "And not for me!"

A cringe spread across Allison's face when she remembered her rash invitation afterward.

The casual offer of friends-with-benefits didn't work at all when voiced. She foolishly counted on two things to happen: One, if accepted, they could have a pleasurable distraction that she felt prepared to handle. And two, if declined, it would have most likely riled him up and made him angry.

Will's response did neither and nipped any ploy for inserting emotional distance between them. And ever since Allison's misplaced step, he had continued to be even more patient with her.

"No. He's sneaky," she acknowledged softly. "Clever enough to strategize that dangling our combustible attraction could hasten my coming around to his way of thinking."

His adamant belief that Allison's love for her sister, Sara, even her uncle, or anyone else—including her new husband—

didn't necessarily seal their fate. "You can't allow fear to keep you from the people you love," he had softly encouraged the other night, holding her in his arms before she fell asleep.

The same message prevailed in her uncle's nightly discussions.

"Damn!" Allison pounded her fist into the firm, dense mattress. Loving him and wanting to stay close was fighting just as vigorously with the need to keep him at arm's length. She rolled to her side, cradling the large, soft damask pillow against her chest.

Naivety to believe that attraction was enough no longer existed. Allison's first marriage cracked that illusion, and her previous attempt with Will obliterated the rest. Plus, other insecurities kept popping up.

Before Rachael got sick, Will described his ex-fiancé as happy to keep things running smoothly at home. In contrast, Allison hated running her uncle's estate and being the perfect hostess at his many political functions.

Allison ripped out the band, holding her hair in a ponytail. Welcoming the slight sting on her scalp, she remembered their first go-a-round. They had only been together for six months, and she had barely recovered from losing him. *But not to a tragic event.* Her conscience argued.

Before thinking Will betrayed her with Nancy, the worry of

Allison's family curse had begun to cause doubts about the direction of the relationship. Anyone looking at Will and her back then–or now–would spot more than the marriage of convenience she had with Mark.

Her secret fantasy was coming true. How long could she keep herself emotionally separate before giving in to the one thing she desperately wanted? This place was beginning to feel like home. And it had nothing to do with the actual building. Being here every day and seeing him with their daughter became both easy and difficult at the same time.

She wished Will would take the decision away from her. He certainly had gained the upper hand in everything else up till now.

"You need to get a grip. Make a decision, go back down, and confront Will!" Her voice echoed around the ample space. One of the smaller pillows got thrown across the room.

Over the last few years, she succeeded in being fair-minded and even-tempered. The lessons from dealing with Senator Buchanan's strong-minded, overly protective, dominant nature molded these attributes to practical use. Becoming a mother to a strong-willed, adventurous child honed those skills even more.

But lately, this seesaw of indecision brought out the worst in her. Her sister, Peggy, even pointed out a solid resemblance to Dr. Jekyll and Mrs. Hyde in one of their many phone conversations. Each frantic call she made to her sister warranted the same given advice. "Talk to your husband. Tell him these fears," Peggy had implored. But Allison continued to argue with everyone.

"Stop this craziness!" Allison sagged against the mountain of pillows left on the bed when the urge to confront him suddenly stopped.

"Is Will strong enough to break a family curse?" she softly cried.

Chapter Twelve

Sean Patterson took the turn-off from Spring Mill Avenue onto Lime Street. The volume of commute flowing around Conshohocken had long dwindled down. Just a few lingering worker-bees staying late to stay ahead of their workload were calling it a day, mixing with the locals' everyday comings and goings.

The Guardians Inc.'s corporate headquarters was positioned at the southeast corner of the city, a stone's throw away from the Schuylkill River. This location showed more foot traffic than other parts due to the many walking paths along the waterway and nearby parks.

"When is the changing of the guards going to take place?" Rebecca Patterson sighed while watching a spirited labradoodle take its owner on a jostling walk just beyond her passenger window. Her presence... and, more importantly, her oldest brother's appearance in this minor assignment required stealth.

No one from the Sons of Liberty could know about their involvement.

"We have over an hour before Matthew's team is scheduled to arrive," James Patterson said, leaning toward the gap between the driver and passenger's seat. This secret snatch took him far from where the Sons of Liberty believed him to be. But the fake trip set up by Sean's hacking magic would pass scrutiny from any of those lurking eyes, giving James a few days before anyone noticed his absence.

The borrowed van held one more row of black vinyl crew seats behind him. They were currently empty. But hopefully, not for long.

Sean eased the vehicle beside the card reader's kiosk. Pressing down on the window control made his glass lower with a slight hum. His security badge quickly got swiped along the reader's pad and released the lock of the parking lot's visitor's gate. Having been a frequent visitor over the years made his visit today uneventful.

Even today's van gave no raised eyebrows or curious glances since he often arrived with multiple computers and security equipment to occasionally drop off or pick up.

The stationed security outbuilding housed two guards. Both of whom Sean recognized as they stepped outside to greet him. "Sean, we didn't have you on the visitor's list for today," the older guard said, leaning against Sean's car door. His gaze quickly surveyed the other two passengers.

"Yeah, my bad, Art. I'm on the schedule for Thursday, but I have an appointment conflict. I thought I'd swing by now and get the installation done, so I won't have to push it back a few weeks." Sean grinned and swung out his hand toward his passengers. "My sister and brother were able to give me a hand unloading."

The guard laughed. "Free labor," he joked.

Sean chuckled good-naturally and added, "You bet. The best kind."

Art tapped on the van's door several times before pushing away. "No problem. I'll make sure the guest log is corrected. Just let the lead security team inside know if you need anything. Talk to you later."

"Sure thing. Give Shelly my best and tell her she'd better make those special brownies for the next company picnic," Sean said before raising his side window. He gave the younger guard a quick wave and drove through the opening.

Will would have to be notified to scrub the visitor files of their arrival from tonight's list. With Maxwell's computer hacking know-how, Sean knew it shouldn't be an issue. Not that Sean couldn't do it; he just knew Will would prefer doing it himself. Call it a fellow hacker's courtesy that Sean felt inclined to extend.

"Now comes the hard part," Rebecca muttered. She heard her oldest brother sigh loudly before flopping against his seat's backrest.

They took the road curving toward the parking lot entrance to the right of the main structure. This area had low-level outbuildings with adjacent parking lots for all commercial and maintenance equipment. A clever landscape designer strategically placed small-sized tree groupings and shrubs around the outside of the lotted area. This concealed the less aesthetical portions of running a large business from the main public's view.

The left side of the main building featured well-maintained landscaping, interspersed with designated parking sections. These areas were primarily used for temporary employees and regular visitors. This area also provided walking trails that tied into the Schuylkill River's nature trails with their own gated entrances and manned security for foot traffic convenient for employees and visitors alike.

With two sub-ground levels, the parking structure's entrance ramped down before another gate required Sean's access card.

Luckily, it was a quiet visitor's day. Sometimes, even with the working day ending for the 9-5 employees, most other sections of the security business were still in high swing. This made the flow of getting from one place to the next within the complex a challenge.

Fifteen minutes later, they circumvented the two lower levels and parked in Sean's assigned parking space on the upper third level. With his sibling's help, they loaded Sean's equipment into the freight elevator and were on their way.

"Good thing you actually had a shipping scheduled this week," Rebecca commented while pushing the button, releasing the cab's door lock. The elevator door swooshed closed.

"Yeah," Sean agreed. His gaze fell on the cart loaded with computer monitors, CPU devices, and numerous power supplies. "Before we go to the lower level, we can store this cart in one of my equipment closets, and I can come back later to install them. Will doesn't want anyone to know we are moving the prisoners. So, the quicker we get this done, the less time anyone will notice we were here."

James nodded and waited for his brother to select the floor level. Of the twenty stories in the main building, Sean's work mainly occurred on the tenth floor, where all the computer labs were located. When the cab began to move, James' gaze went to Rebecca. "You ready to fly out?"

"Yes, just as soon as I finish here, they have a plane waiting to take me to the Virginia safe house. I met Sara in the morning."

"Okay." James broke eye contact and stared straight ahead. He had major reservations about getting her involved in this case, but they had no choice. The number of people they could trust seemed to be diminishing each day.

His concern wasn't that he thought she couldn't handle herself in the field. She had high scores as a cadet and more than proven herself already as an agent. It had more to do with her being his kid sister, and no matter how much everyone found her competent, James didn't want danger to come anywhere near her.

A low sigh escaped James' lips before his jaw clenched and his lips pressed tightly. Just thinking about the danger she could be exposed to, he wanted him to call the whole mission off.

The cab gave a buzz when reaching the selected level. When the doors opened, Sean stepped out. "Stay here," he ordered while pushing the door lock button again. He tugged on the cart's handle to get it moving. Once it got maneuvered out of the elevator, his gaze fell on his older brother. "I'll get this secured and be right back."

Rebecca anxiously began tapping on the side of her leg, willing her brother back as soon as possible.

"You know, brat. That doesn't actually work." James smirked, recalling when his baby sister used to do the very same thing whenever she wanted to get her way. It had only worked back then because all four of her brothers spoiled her fiercely.

As Sean rushed into the cab's interior, sawing in and out harsh breaths of air, she turned to give James a pointed look. "Yes, it does," she argued.

James chuckled under his breath. Knowing when beaten made it easy to let it go. His gaze watched as the floor levels decreased in number.

He took a deep breath and mentally calculated each step of this impromptu assignment. This portion was the easy part. What came next would serve as more challenging in the grand scheme of things, but he took nothing for granted.

And thankfully, the next part went without a hitch.

The two ex-employees of Guardians Inc. removed from the holding cell, rode the elevator up to the parking lot level in complete silence. Their hands were locked behind their backs with wrist restraints.

No one spoke of what happened in Orlando, Florida.

No one spoke of the prisoners' inquiries about where they were headed or what happened when they got there.

But a lot was riding on someone providing answers.

Will asked Sean to move these men before the FBI team came to collect them and didn't want anyone to know where they ended up. With all the moles in their ranks, the Guardians Inc.'s CEO didn't want to hand them over to just anybody. With the Sons of Liberty's prisoners getting released or killed, he didn't want to take the chance that these men might disappear, too.

Not before Will and the Patterson brothers got their answers. After those questions were resolved, only then would Will risk giving them away. After that, he didn't give a damn about their disappearance.

When the freight elevator came to the same floor as Patterson's van, the interior cab jolted to a stop. James led the men out, with Sean and Rebecca following up the rear.

Sean moved forward to get the van doors unlocked, and Rebecca went to the passenger side like before. But as they approached the corner, a loud slam of a car door closing was heard followed by an explosion of movement.

Jennifer Daniels, wearing a Guardians Inc.'s security uniform, raced between James Patterson and the two Guardians Inc. betrayers from behind. She quickly inserted a syringe into James' shoulder and pressed down. Within moments, the drug coursed through his blood and dropped the oldest Patterson brother unharmed to the concrete floor and slipped a folded business card into his back pocket.

She had just a moment to spray a misted aerosol sedative toward the two incarcerated men before fielding any reciprocating attacks. This had the same effect as before, and the two men dropped unconscious quickly.

Rebecca came around the side of the van and witnessed her oldest brother fall to the ground. She shouted her dismay and came running to his aid.

A yell off to the side made her glance back to see her brother, Sean, fighting an older man.

Micheal Arnald, also dressed as a security guard, struggled with a hypodermic needle while fighting the younger brother. But all too soon, the seasoned agent sent an under-sweeping kick to the younger man's legs, making his quarry fall backward.

Swooping in, he got the needle stabbed in Sean's leg, and within seconds, the drug took another Patterson brother under.

With a warrior's battle cry, Rebecca went to attack the older man, but the slim-framed female intercepted her with a round-house kick.

Jennifer Daniels' assault caused Rebecca to arc back. The attacking movement's breeze brushed against Rebecca's face before she quickly centered her frame, readying a fighter's stance. Rebecca's counterattack of a forward jab caught the other woman's shoulder before dodging an offensive swing. The two women looked evenly matched, and each strike was equally returned in the same spirited manner. Neither spared the other in holding back their hits or the strength behind each attack.

"They're unharmed, you know," Jennifer Daniels calmly stated while effortlessly blocking her opponent's attack. She brought her knee up, then thrust it forward with force, gaining momentum for her next kick. The kick went wide, and she had to block her opponent's next attack quickly.

Michael Arenald saw the fighting for what it was: a distraction. He quickly moved to the unconscious Guardians Inc.'s prisoners lying on the ground.

The mist spray was fast-acting but quickly burned through the victim's system. They wouldn't have much time to secure them before the sedative wore off. Dragging the larger framed individual proved cumbersome, but Michael had dealt with more demanding situations. He kept an eye on Jennifer, using her altercation with the youngest Patterson as an opportunity to get them ready to move.

"It is nothing more than a fast-acting sedative. Your brothers will awake without any ill effects." Jennifer realized the time to wrap this fight up came to a point. She swung her arm, sweeping a push to the underside of Rebecca's knees. This move unbalanced the young agent, causing her to tilt backward. Jennifer followed up with a rounding kick, and Rebecca fell to the ground.

Hitting the ground hard made her wince in pain. But her worry was centered more on her brothers than herself.

Jennifer Daniels stood over the fallen Patterson sibling. A pointed gun in hand gave her order to stay down some added weight. The Sons of Liberty's agent stepped back when Rebecca submitted with her palms held out. With a glance, she spotted Micheal getting the last prisoner in their vehicle.

"Until we meet again, Agent Patterson," Ms. Daniels said pleasantly. She moved her hand, gesturing as if tipping a hat at Rebecca before backing away. "I'm sure the next time will be as equally riveting."

And with that parting shot, she darted backward, jumped into the waiting car, and drove away.

Rebecca slammed her palms against the polished concrete floor with a defeated look.

Their enemy always seemed to be two steps ahead of them.

She quickly moved toward her brother Sean. Never was she more frustrated in having her healing ability non-operational. She could have easily pushed the sedative's effects from both of her brother's bodies if it had been possible. But since that fateful night years ago, her more dominate ability didn't work.

Touching an area on Sean's neck indicated a regular pulse. Her gaze turned to James, who looked to be rousing awake. Jennifer Daniels had been telling the truth, it seemed.

A loud groan echoed from James' mouth.

Rebecca carefully positioned Sean in a sitting position, leaning him against the van with the open door. She repeatedly patted her brother's cheek. As he began to frown, trying to pull away, she knew it wouldn't be long before the drug mostly left his system, too.

Sighing softly, she knew this situation didn't make a good first impression for her transfer to Maxwell's safe house. She also wondered how Will Maxwell would react when he'd realize more questions would go unanswered. Yet again.

Chapter Thirteen

At the same moment as Patterson's attack, Will Maxwell opened his bedroom door at Virginia's safe house. He was whistling and rubbing his hair dry with a brightly colored beach towel, when entering the room.

Not realizing his failed attempt to keep Guardians Inc.'s ex-employees out of the FBI's hands could explain this good mood.

All his attention was centered on his wife lying on their bed.

Allison swiveled herself around to face him and swore under her breath.

Crossing the room, stopping at his dresser, he opened several drawers and picked out various articles of clothing. He acted utterly unaware of–or ignored–her sulking presence.

"Just what do you think you're doing, Buster?"

Angling off from the piece of furniture, a pair of socks and shorts in one hand, the towel he used to dry off presently draped across his one shoulder, Will faced the most beautiful, angriest, and sexiest female he had ever known.

Allison stayed kneeling in the middle of their bed with her forefinger pointed straight at him. He would be a dead man if she could shoot lightning right now.

Thinking maybe he was taking this a little too far, Will briefly questioned his tactics while simultaneously appreciating their present results.

Allison's temper elicited a nice effect on her scantily covered body. With her cover-up's belt undone, she flashed enticing views that her husband soaked in.

Her breasts, displayed snugly in her bikini top, rose and fell at an increased rate, showing off ample cleavage. A tight abdomen from her habitual running routine clenched even tighter with frustration and raw energy. Shapely thighs shifting to maintain her balance on the plush, dense mattress accentuated her toned physique to perfection.

Her face reflected raw passion and longing, and he briefly wondered if she realized how much she was giving away before holding firm to his cause. It felt like her eyes shot piercing green flames of fire directly to his erection. But he kept the calm, relaxed expression he had adopted these past days–which felt like it was slowly killing him–and stepped onto the battlefield.

All is fair in love and war. His thoughts acknowledged, and knowing it would put her over the edge, he asked, "What?"

She jumped up from kneeling and stomped across the room to stand before him. "What. Do. You. Think. You're doing?" Each word got punctuated with a point of her finger poking his bare chest.

"Getting changed. You know... from being in the pool, swimming, and playing with Sara."

Allison remembered that quite vividly. It became the very reason she had excused herself from the games and came up here. With the warmer weather and the pool heated, Will's suggestion became the only thing Sara wanted to do.

There had been no other possible activities that would measure up. And knowing the byproduct of that particular activity, Allison had adamantly tried otherwise. And, of course, she had been right.

Will, in his swimming trunks, playing had been just too much for Allison to handle. Especially since he kept bumping against her in the water while catching the volleyball, Sara tossed their way.

For a moment, Allison had sworn a smirk appeared on his handsome face, along with glittering flashes reflected in his gaze before innocent enjoyment replaced it in the blink of an eye.

"Why aren't you down there? You know very well that Sara will go in the deep end!" she practically screamed in his face. She couldn't seem to help it. Dr. Jekyll was raring to go.

"Allison, you know very well that I wouldn't leave Sara alone by the pool. Pete came out to tell us lunch was ready; He is fine watching our daughter while I get changed. In fact- I'm going right back down there to join them. You coming?"

Spinning away from her, he hid a grin.

Heading for the connecting door to Sara's room, he mentioned, "Sara had pitched a fit wanting to keep wearing her swimsuit. So, I compromised and told her wearing a robe would work for lunch," he calmly added.

Allison marched to intercept. "What? You're just going to leave without discussing this?"

"Discuss what, Allison?" Will eased around and continued, "You need to learn to relax, sweetheart. It won't do Sara any good seeing you like this." While talking, he gently guided her back to their bed. "Exercise is just the thing. I'll tell Jeff and Pete to go ahead with lunch and feed Sara. I'll postpone the report meeting so we can workout together. Sound like a plan?"

She whipped his casual hand away from her back. "No! It's not okay, Will. Do you hear me? I don't want to be calm about this! I... I need to decide on something- I did decide on it earlier, but then you waltzed in here like that-" She waved a hand at his appearance. "And now I'm not sure if it's the right one. But I need to make a decision and stick with it!"

"What, Ally? What do you need to decide?" Will prompted. Dealing with those grappling uncertainties, Allison became too far gone to notice Will having gone still and alert.

Pacing back and forth in front of the bed, she tried to deny what she wanted most.

Will decided to push the envelope further. "I can ask Debbie and Jake to send some work down here. I can ensure no trace back to this location."

Allison stomped her foot down on the thick, plush carpet. "You're driving me-" Looking at him-as her emotional barriers broke down-Allison stopped letting fear be an excuse. "It's not about work. I don't want to exercise. I just-"

Allison paused. There would be no going back if she said it to him.

You can do it, baby-just say it. Will urged her.

"I, I love you too." The words spilled out of Allison's mouth in a rush of panic. "Even when this is over. I want to be with you. Oh God! But I'm afraid. What if I lose you?"

Thank you, God! Will silently shouted before sweeping Allison up-off her feet-and carrying her to their bed. These past few nights of not touching her had wreaked havoc on any chance of a restful sleep.

Allison wrapped her arms around Will's shoulders, hugging his body tightly. Will climbed onto the bed and knelt on the mattress with her still cradled in his arms. "Tell me you want this. Tell me you want us together.

"Tell me," he demanded again, shaking her gently. He needed to hear the words.

"You-" she admitted with eyes full of love and need. "I want to stay with you." She moved her hands, sinking her fingers into his unruly hair, guiding his lips down to her.

He moaned with pent-up frustration, seeking a release from this burning obsession to consume her with his mouth, hands, and body. No one else could elicit such a need as this from him. Just Allison. He broke contact briefly when the call for air in his lungs won over his need for her. But that didn't stop him for long.

Dropping her, Will ignored Allison's gasp as she fell onto the plush pillows. A small payback for all she had put them both through these last few days. Will straddled her waist, leaning over her. Looking as if he wandered lost in the desert for days without water–and she was a cool, clear fountain–he wanted to consume.

Allison's hands explored his back, molding and massaging

the hard lines of his muscles. Tracing the path down to his spine; she grew excited by the strength and hardness of his contours. When fabric impeded her from getting more skin, she moaned in disappointment, delayed from her goal.

She immediately brought her fingers to the band of his swim trunks, teasing him by slipping inside and slowly retreating.

Her husband growled and then reciprocated in his own way. With his torso lifted from her, he lowered his mouth to brush against one perked nipple under the stretchy material, then moved to the next.

Squirming with anticipation, wanting more of this pleasure, she tried to pull him closer. Her breasts felt heavy and sensitive from his attention.

However, he moved and brought his mouth close to her ear. "Touch me, and then I'll touch you," he promised in a guttural voice.

Will wasn't the only one trying to hold onto some semblance of control and failing. Allison leaned up and untied the string to his bathing trunks with shaking hands. With one eyebrow raised, she slowly eased them down.

He kicked the interfering barrier off and started following through on his promise but got distracted. Allison went to undo her bikini top, but Will quickly interjected, "I want the top left on." Knowing what little control he had left would be lost if she removed that particular barrier.

His mouth roamed her lips, cheeks, and eyes before trailing to the area behind her ear.

Allison sucked in sharply when Will knowingly hit that sensitive spot.

Lowering himself closer, he grabbed her hands in one of his and repositioned them above her head. He reached for the bikini bottoms with his free hand and nimbly tugged them past her hips and down her legs. He settled fully on top of her.

She relished in the weight of him pressing her down. His desperate need felt rigid against her stomach. His mouth sought her throat, lavishing open-mouthed kisses along her jawline, collarbone, and the highly erogenous area behind her ear, making her body burn.

His lower spine became explored with busy hands. Stroking fingertips trailed along the dip above the buttocks, concentrating on one particular area that always brought him to the edge when he'd been inside her. His body shuddered.

Her mind was flooded with telepathic images of his intentions and what he wanted to do to her. Her body trembled with anticipation.

Will raised himself slightly over her, just enough to allow

her hand access to where he craved her touch. His mouth moved slowly down from her throat. He trailed open-mouth kisses, gentle nips, and tormenting licks on her sensitive skin, resulting in a multitude of tingling sensations of pleasure. A hot, stroking tongue followed a path from the string holding up her bikini top to the thin barrier of silky fabric covering her breast.

A tide of sensations laid siege over her. Allison's body arched upward. She moaned and raised one hand, clasping his neck to keep his mouth where she needed him to stay.

He chuckled, lifted his head, and took in the vision under him.

God, how captivatingly beautiful.

Allison's eyes remained dazed and unfocused. Her cheeks flushed pink with passion. Her mouth was plump and wet from their lovemaking. She was so caught up in the sensual bombardment that she became impatient and demanding. These feelings only ever rose inside her when she was with Will.

Her only other lover, Mark, her ex-husband, never caused her to lose herself in pleasure like this and called her many unflattering names because of it. Thinking herself flawed, she had wanted no other man to follow afterward.

But then Will came into her life, and everything changed.

Only he could evoke this mindless need.

Whimpering softly, she urged him on with her hands and body. A sensual rocking of her hips urged their bodies to join together.

"Soon," Will whispered.

Chapter Fourteen

"N o. Right now!" Allison demanded. Clever touches became determined seduction, seeking to destroy his control. Her legs wrapped around his hips, guiding him to her.

She had become the conqueror.

"Baby, let me get a condom," Will whispered while trying to pull away.

No, have IUD. She projected her thoughts to him while pulling his body closer.

Will lost what little control he had left. A primitive growl rumbled deep within his chest when he slowly entered her tight channel.

They both groaned in pleasure from their joining.

Allison grasped tightly onto his hips–to pull him even closer.

Will was overwhelmed by sensation as his head lowered uncontrollably. The muscles gripping him, squeezed him drawing him in deeper. His chin dropped to his chest, and waves of pleasure hit him, making him crave the taste of her skin. He kissed one breast, then the other, while his hips moved rhythmically with hers.

The sole purpose of pushing her over the edge became like a drum beating in his soul.

Finesse, gentleness, and control gave way to pure, undiluted greed.

Allison matched Will's rhythm. Letting go of his hips, realizing the pinnacle drew nearer, she stroked the curve of his spine, sending them both flying. With a cry escaping their lips, they lost themselves in the soaring pleasures of their mating.

Becoming one. Their union truly consummated. The separate thread of each heart, tethering their souls together, fused to an unbreakable, glittering mating bond.

As their heartbeats slowed, their breathing also returned to normal. The room had a soft, warm glow, like the sun's rays after a passing storm. "Tell me. Tell me again," Will whispered while stroking her shoulder and lower back as the world settled on its axis.

Cuddling closer to his chest, she said. "I love you so much, Will."

He tilted his head slightly to watch her face and gently

moved the curl that shielded her eyes from full view. He watched in awe as a beautifully tender smile appeared.

"What is it?" he asked.

"I feel whole," Allison simply answered, and then, sighing, gave in to the pull to sleep.

With one of her legs tucked intimately between his, Allison's head laid to the side, with her cheek and hands resting on his chest. Small puffs of warm breath moved his chest hair and eased his heart rate to match the rhythm of hers.

Will knew Allison's precise meaning. This subtle but firm tether to this woman–his woman–was what he had been fighting all these years.

Funny, how I thought it would hinder me, make me weak.

I've been such a fool. Will admitted to himself, realizing Allison made his life feel–complete.

Now, the only thing to make right was telling his wife about his involvement with her uncle. His confidence in his persuasive technique made him cocky when usually caution served a better path.

Will carefully untied the strings to her bikini top, tugged it from between them, and threw it across the bed. While falling asleep, he had a smug smile on his lips.

****

"Allison," Senator Buchanan called to his niece. He stepped through the portal of the dreamscape he had created and sat on the edge of her bed. It had become even more urgent that he get through to her about staying with William Maxwell.

Watching as her eyes flickered open and connected with him, his heart just about broke when fear became the first emotion shown on her expressive face. He knew he couldn't change the past, but deep regrets that their relationship suffered consequences over the need to keep her safe plagued him.

"Uncle," Allison said while sitting up in the hospital bed. The room was a replica of the one she had spent time in during a college break after the plane crash when everything changed between them.

As the wariness faded from her eyes, he held tight to the hope that she still wanted a relationship with him despite everything that happened. There was a chance to repair the damage and have another opportunity to protect her.

This time, however, he wouldn't push her away.

"Honey, I won't have the chance to visit again for some time. You must believe what I'm saying to you." His hand clasped one of hers and squeezed briefly. The urgency of the approaching situation locked him in a deep panic.

Allison swung herself out from under the covers, sitting on

the bed with her legs draped over the edge. "I don't know why I keep dreaming this scene over and over with you," she whispered.

He shook his head quickly in disagreement. "Sweetheart, this is not a normal dream. This is a dream-link. Everything I say is real. It is not part of your sub-conscience or wishful thinking," he urged her to believe. "How can I prove to you it is true?"

His eyes darted away to focus on the opposite wall. The surfaces moved and shifted like viewing the backdrop through a heavy fog. He clenched his jaw before swinging his gaze back on Allison.

"I do have something. But it may hinder my case instead of helping it," he warned, adding, "Before I tell you, I want your promise that you and Sara stay close to Will. No matter what I may say outside of this dream-link. You and William Maxwell are stronger when you stand together." He emphasized his point by grasping her hand and gently squeezing it.

"Promise me," he demanded.

"I promise," Allison whispered while her gaze was focused on their clasped hands.

He felt her pulling from the dream, severing his connection. He nodded once, and the palm of his free hand smoothed down the fabric on his upper thighs before he continued, "When you left home to live in the Conshohocken townhouse, I had Will watching over you. But I hired Guardians, Inc. to shadow you after you two broke up. Your sister, too. I asked him to keep it to himself and sign a NDA.

"Ask Will if it is true. Then, ask yourself, how would this be possible to dream of if you didn't know anything about it?"

"Remember your promise," her uncle urged while he and the room faded into nothingness.

****

Will slammed down the phone and swore under his breath. The loose, relaxed manner in which he entered the library a few moments ago fled like a bullet fired from a gun.

He was thankful that the Patterson brothers were recovering from their attack and sequential drugging. Plus, Rebecca, although sore, was unharmed and en route to the safe house. But the news Sean shared was the opposite of what he wanted to hear.

It seemed James' presence at the prisoners' exchange could jeopardize his undercover assignment within the Sons of Liberty.

His fingers roughly combed through his disheveled hair, and a heavy sigh escaped his lips. What he had asked of them could now set them back again in this never-ending investigation.

After what happened at the Orlando site, Will had triple-checked his men and women among the upper-security tiers. However, they were counting on getting information from those ex-employees about the other traitors among the Guardians Inc.'s personnel.

"It was a long shot to secure the men from the FBI's reach," Jeff commented. Even though he worked directly for them, he agreed with Will that the Guardians Inc.'s contacts would prove more secure. Since each prisoner in the FBI's care didn't fare so well.

They were both just proven wrong.

"We can't catch a break," Will exclaimed.

"Well, there is nothing we can do about it now. I'll tell the higher-ups that a security breach occurred before Matthew's team arrived. We'll have to review your employee list again," Jeff mentioned before, slapping Will on the back.

"Go! Be with your bride," He urged his best friend. "Or you'll have hell to pay for abandoning her after..." His hand twirled in a waving manner. "You know," he said with a smirk.

"I do know," Will replied. A wide grin returned across his face. A good-natured slap on Jeff's back proceeded Will's quick departure from the room.

He had a wedding night to celebrate. Rushing back to their bedroom, Will couldn't get to his bride fast enough.

Allison slowly surfaced from a deep slumber. She shifted and glided her hand across the cold sheets on the opposite side of the bed. When feeling the emptiness beside her, she woke fully.

"What a strange dream," she said. A vague memory of talking with her uncle lay just out of reach in her mind.

Sitting up, she looked around the room. With the presence of sharp shadows in the room, it seemed to be late afternoon. Her watch confirmed her assumption when she read 4:00 p.m. Angling back to the empty pillow beside hers, she quickly saw what her husband left behind.

Easing down onto her side and reaching for the paper, she read his note:

Ally,

Had to take care of a bit of work.

Jeff is on Sara's duty until tomorrow.

I'll be back as soon as I'm done.

Do not get out of this bed!

Love you, W

Rolling onto her back, Allison sighed dreamily, like a schoolgirl. She stretched out her arms. Even though her body gave twinges, sore in some areas due to their passionate lovemaking; she had never felt better.

The dream message from her uncle faded further away.

A laugh in delight passed through her smiling lips when a deviously delightful idea popped into her head. She jumped up and headed into the bathroom. She went to the whirlpool, turned the dial toward hot, and the water spouted from the faucet. Spotting the large container of bubble bath, she felt thrilled. A heavy-handed approach proceeded to dump some of the bottle's contents into the swirling water before she stepped into the hot, bubbling tub.

Allison hummed softly. It was time for the Ranger to get some of what he had dished out.

With their stronger physical and emotional connection came a stronger telepathic bond. She immediately sensed when Will entered their suite. She proceeded to pour more bath lotion directly onto her skin.

As the bathroom door opened, Allison slowly rose out of the water. The sensations of bubbles gliding down her body caressed her skin. Her hands reached up, releasing the clip that held her hair in a loose bun. Dark, silky waves tumbled artistically down, covering portions of her anatomy from his hungry eyes.

She felt beautiful, posing for him.

Hearing his soft inhale of breath, she slowly lowered her body to the water.

With her arched back, locks of hair cascaded down into the pooling water, exposing her soft silky breasts and upper torso slick with a glossy film. Will let his eyes devour it all. Spellbound, he watched as she inhaled, held her breath, and sank below the warm, pulsating water.

He had a towel ready when she broke through the water's surface, gently wiping the soapy water off her face, revealing her tempting smile.

Resembling Eve in the garden, she said, "Hi, Ranger. Wanna wash my back?" She let her fingers trail across her upper body, disturbing a trail of soapy bubbles and exposing more of her body to his gaze. Raising her arms, making a production as she bent them behind her head, she stroked her fingers along her slippery skin. Her eyelashes batting playfully for him.

"Of course, love." Eagerly playing along, he lowered himself to sit on the edge. "Close your eyes and relax." His hands guided her to sit fully upright.

Feeling his limbs wrap around her from behind, she opened her eyes in playful shock. "But you were supposed to stay out there." She pointed to the spot when their roles were reversed, and she had been the one giving the massage.

"Well, Ally." Will's fingers began their seduction by softly caressing her neck and shoulder blades. He felt Allison shiver. "I had to give this problem my full attention."

Grabbing her hips, he brought her closer to his heavy erection. "Now, just close your eyes and relax. Let me get to work." His hands touched her everywhere. The need to claim her again rode him hard.

A few steamy moments later, Allison had difficulties finding her voice. "Um... Will?"

"Hmm..." He responded as he nuzzled her head to one side, providing better access to one of her sensitive areas. Even with the fragrance of the bathing gel, her unique scent of Apple Blossoms drove him on. He licked some bubbles away, causing wave after wave of tremors through her body.

"I don't feel very relaxed," she breathily spoke.

Her warm, slippery skin slid against him. The press of her body increased as she turned in his embrace. Opening his eyes, he focused on her glistening breast facing him. "How do you feel?"

"Very excited," she whispered in his ear, biting his lobe. "In fact- I think the only way for me to loosen up is to do this-" She licked behind his ear. "Ahh... and this." She caressed his shoulders and upper back. "And most certainly... this."

But before Allison's hands could finish their path down his

chest, he held them in place with his. "Allison?" Will growled in tight restraint.

"Hmm," she purred.

"Get prepared to feel very, very relaxed." He swept them both down into the water and let the bubbles fly.

Chapter Fifteen

The following evening, Michael Arenald stepped into the basement holding cell of a Delaware City townhouse. The property's importance was solely related to its proximity to the ferry terminal that traveled back and forth from Pea Patch Island.

The battered-looking occupant in the room adjusted his stance. His bandaged shoulder wound seeped with fresh blood from recent exertion. A chain that secured him to the poured concrete foundation made a dragging sound as the metal links scraped along the hard-surfaced floor. The wrist holding him to his chained mooring showed evidence of his struggle to break free.

Turning his back on the captive man to watch as another entered the room, Michael sighed heavily as a smirk spread across his associate's face. "Don't look at me like that," he spoke softly. His posh-like accent gave way to a more common Cockney dialect used by East Londoners. A more telling sign of his ire couldn't be found. He pulled off his dark gray cap and placed it on the wooden chair's seat next to the door. Too far away from the length of the chain to access. His customary uniform's gray blazer went next and got hung on the chair's high back.

"Like what? Oh… maybe, how you may look at someone who tried to kill him?" Michael's associate had no jacket to fold neatly, but he did roll up the crisp sleeves of his pressed shirt.

"MJ, quit your bollocking. We need information from this guy about the warehouse attack. And the chance we took in exposing ourselves to the Pattersons has to pay-off with the other two from Maxwell's company waiting next.

"I can get them to talk," Michael softly spoke. He glanced at MJ while tilting his chin toward their nearby captive. "But you're the fastest at filtering through their lies." Michael's gaze leveled on the prisoner when he heard him gasp. As the man's eyes widened in shock, Black's chauffeur moved closer.

"You're supposed to be dead," the captive man said in disbelief, looking toward MJ. He acted as if he had seen a ghost. "Sharpe said he tossed you in the New River."

Miles Jenning sauntered inside, closing the door behind him. "No worries, mate. I know it was nothing personal," he muttered while passing by his new partner. Neither man liked the recent arrangement.

"For Bloody sake!" Michael shifted his stance to address MJ. "I already explained. We didn't warn you to make it look real. Don't you think the fact that you can come back from the dead warranted Black's decision?" His voice spoke swiftly, but he made sure to prevent anyone from overhearing.

MJ could feel the heat from his counterpart's breath brush his face and became instantly thankful for Michael's fondness of those mint-flavored, hard candies. "Oh, sod off. I'm sure it did. I just wanted you to admit that you probably Bloody well enjoyed shooting me." MJ smirked again and then turned to study their lead on the case.

"Okay. Playtime is over. Let's get down to business. We need to know where Sharpe is veering off from the plan," MJ said while heading toward their first prisoner.

****

The lower-level gym stood empty and quiet at the safe house in West Virginia.

"Good. I have it all to myself," Rebecca Patterson sighed, stepping into the room. The large, pimped-out gym systematically turned on the lights when her presence tripped the motion detector's sensors.

Having arrived late last night, she missed the opportunity to set a bedtime routine with her young charge. Meeting Sara this morning only reaffirmed her belief that the child thrived in a structured schedule. Like most children, she found repetition comforting.

Unfortunately, another opportunity to set a bedtime groove went undone. Allison wanted to put Sara to bed tonight since mother and daughter had spent little time together last night and this morning.

This allowed the nanny/bodyguard some free time. Having downtime so soon into her assignment felt strange; and Rebecca had wished to avoid having any at all. She didn't want to have time to dwell on why she was here.

But hopefully, getting some physical activity in now would help keep her mind off those things.

Pairing her earpods with her phone, she blasted the music loud enough to drown out her thoughts. Her slight frame stepped onto the nearest treadmill.

An hour and seven and a half miles later, short of breath and soaked from heavy exertion, Rebecca took a long draw from the thawing water bottle and headed to the center of the exercise mat.

The bottle was placed aside as her real workout began. Her movements, though fluid and graceful, got mixed with a bit of roughness due to the music's beat. The soreness from fighting a round or two with the Sons of Liberty's female agent slowly faded. If an opportunity for some payback came around, Rebecca wanted to be ready.

The fast, deep drumming of hip-hop always helped in keeping her motivated. The hard beat matched in time with the high kicks and firm jabs on the sparring body bag left for occasions like this. She may look like a heavy breeze would blow her away, but her 5'-10" toned frame packed a wallop of strength and an attitude to match.

Jeff walked in and stopped dead at the entrance, feeling like a voyeur watching her kick the shit out of the dummy. *Damn it, I don't need this shit right now.*

His absorbing focus caused an area of his body to stand at attention that presently lacked sufficient coverage to hide.

This wasn't his plan when thinking a workout before Will's training would do him good. It would be a mistake to get drawn in by the energy of this slip of a woman. He couldn't afford a distraction.

Knowing when to retreat, he turned to leave when she called out.

"Almost finished. I can get out of your way." Rebecca bent over, catching her breath, when he angled back around to face her. The sports bra and colorful tank top pressed tightly to her slight frame held dips and curves that would've caught any man's attention. But his eyes noticed the faint bruising along her neck and shoulder.

She took off her earbuds and reached for her bottle.

This time, Jeff watched her throat ripple with every pull of liquid she took, drawing his attention to the beads of moisture escaping her mouth and slowly rolling down her throat to get lost in the valley between her breasts. The insane urge to put his lips there and suck overtook him.

"That's okay; take your time. I'm just waiting on Will for a sparring session."

"Oh, do you mind if I stay and watch?" As much as he made her uncomfortable, she shouldn't turn down the opportunity to see how he fought. And she knew well enough that words in a report could be falsified. Plus, the last time they saw each other, he had pretended to be a college professor.

A foolish thought popped into Jeff's mind. *It could be a mistake, but what the hell?*

He smirked before saying, "I'll do one better. I need to warm up, and it seems you're already there. How about sparring with me until Will gets here?" Seeing her in action became a hell of a lot better idea than reading about it and taking Sean Patterson's word for it. Personal feelings aside–he couldn't take the chance that they got the information wrong.

Oh, this is going to be fun!

Her thoughts projected into Jeff's mind before her shields blocked further communications. Her smile turned sly. Pulling out her phone from its snug, resting place–between her lower back and tight-fitting exercise capris–she held it in hand while removing the Wi-Fi-linked earpods with the other. Both items got put with her water bottle and towel out of their way.

Jeff came forward, kicked the lever exposing the industrial casters, and moved the exercise dummy–affectionately dubbed Chuck–out of the way.

They both met back in the center of the mat, facing each other.

An offensive maneuver came at her quickly, and she countered just as fast. He moved, not holding back despite her recent attack. He tested her limits, striking out in fluidly aggressive attacks.

Yet, getting back at her for all the unwanted complications she caused was an unexpected bonus.

This gifted time he gave himself, working off some unwanted frustration before Will's session went by in a blink of an eye. It didn't matter that he was now enjoying the very company he had been trying to avoid.

It was hard to believe she'd ever fallen for his professor's alias, especially now that he moved so aggressively, displaying his warrior-like prowess.

So far, she held her own in this match, but she had a feeling he was testing her and not going all-out.

Besides the extensive workout before his appearance, her short recovery from yesterday's events had begun to deplete her strength. She needed to quit fooling around and get him on the defensive, or she would be done for.

Faking right, she swung left and held his arm to support her weight while wrapping her body around his back to kick out his leg from behind. Stealing one of Jennifer Daniels' maneuvers, Rebecca improvised. Using her body weight and momentum, she tipped him over.

As he fell backward, she pushed off, curled, and landed in a handstand, flipping back to straddle his chest. By Jeff's grinning face looking up at her, Rebecca could see he clearly enjoyed playing with her.

Using his upper torso as a springboard and gripping her thighs, he flipped her forward. Using the strength in his arms, he threw her legs over her body in an overhead tumble.

She landed hard on her back and got the air knocked out of her lungs.

Jeff rolled onto his stomach, pushed off with his arms, and jumped to stand by her side. He concentrated on getting air into his lungs. "Had enou... ff-"

Her response put him on the ground before his question ended. Two rapid kicks to his chest got her off the mat, followed by a kick very close to his groin that had him sucking in oxygen.

"Now. I think I've had enough." She backed up, slowly heading for her stuff. By the look on his face, she would pay for that move one way or another.

Shooting out a hand, he caught her foot and pulled her closer. Anticipating her response, he dove under the swing of her free leg. As he rolled onto his back, he used her forward momentum to sweep her foot out from under her.

While she fell, he grabbed her hands and kept them captive in one of his. He swung her around to land hard on her stomach, leaving her unable to counter his attack. Pressing her hands tight to her lower back, he straddled her waist and lowered his mouth to her ear. "Say, Uncle, Paddlepus." His harsh breathing made his voice sound deep and low.

Rebecca tried to move, but he was not as light as he looked.

His hard, heavily muscular thighs pressed tightly to her hips, and the heavy press of his chest kept her in place.

She had hit the mat face down, causing her to bite her lip. Rolling her head to the side with her cheek resting on the mat, she licked the blood from her lips. Her heart drummed so fast she feared it would pop out of her chest.

Jeff watched as she licked her lips. Satisfaction and possessive emotions swirled around him. Drawn to her mouth, he licked, sucked, and demanded another kind of surrender.

And Rebecca gave it to him.

He immediately released her hands. Leaning forward, he moved his hands to either side of her head making it possible to take more of her sweetness.

Feeling his erection swell in the palms of her hand, Rebecca massaged and erotically squeezed, shooting the heat in him to an inferno degree. His kiss became fiercely driven to make sure she got equally affected.

Will stood leaning against the door frame; a towel swung around his neck with his hands grasping each end. "If this is some new self-defense move I'm not aware of, I got to say, Jeff, I'm gonna pass on our lesson."

The two people on the mat froze. Their panting breaths

mingled together.

Jeff jumped up first, hesitating, before reaching out his hand toward Rebecca. She grasped on, and he pulled her close to his body. He still had to fight the urge to continue their kiss.

Facing away from Will, Rebecca tucked her head down to shield her emotions from the man standing so close. She could still feel the sweltering desire pouring off his body and hers. She attempted to move around him, but his hand on her arm delayed her exit.

"This was a mistake- I'm sorry," Jeff softly spoke. His closed expression was unreadable.

"Yeah. Well, professor, it's certainly not the first time you've regretted your actions after the fact. I survived the last time. I'm sure I will again." She stepped away, scooped up her things on the bench, and hastily retreated.

Will moved away from the door and watched as she approached. When he went to open his mouth to talk, she fervently shook her head no. Deciding to leave it alone for now, Will nodded and let her pass.

"Well. To say I'm not surprised would be a lie," Will commented as he entered the room. "What the hell. Do you think that is wise?"

"Screw you." Jeff stepped away, reaching for the water container Rebecca had left behind. He zealously emptied the rest of the bottle. He was burning alive from the inside out, and the water didn't come close to extinguishing the flames.

Chapter Sixteen

L ater that night, Will had news to share with his bride.

Wanting his life back—a life with his wife and daughter—he would do anything to make it happen. With the realization that James Pattersons' cover could be blown at any minute, they had to shake things up. Which meant this investigation needed to be over sooner rather than later. And an opportunity to see it through had presented itself, and he wouldn't let it pass.

He struggled to find a way to tell Allison he would be leaving in the morning.

Opening the door to their bedroom quietly, he walked through the threshold and stopped just inside the opening. A scent tickled his senses. The smell of Apple Blossoms seeped into his nose and filled his lungs. He inhaled deeply, wanting more.

Allison sat up in bed, aimlessly flipping through a magazine. Her eyes lifted, and their gazes locked.

"I'll be right back," he said, heading for the bathroom.

The sound of a nearby faucet in use filled the quiet space in the suite's adjoining room. After a few moments, the rushing water stopped, and a stillness remained. Allison scooted closer to Will's side of the bed, preparing for his return. With their linked connection, she felt her husband's unease, but he kept his thoughts locked behind a shield she couldn't breach even if she tried.

The rigid body stance and lip-biting clearly hinted to her approaching husband of an upcoming skirmish. Her gaze studied him as he smiled, flipped back the covers, and got into bed. His chilled body immediately stole some of her warmth.

Nope. Will decided, pushing his exhale out and shoring up his mental shields. *This will not go well.*

As his weight dipped the mattress, bringing her closer, Allison could smell the mint of his toothpaste. He leaned into her, tucking a stray curl behind her ear, and kissed her softly.

When he pulled back to speak, Allison beat him to the punch. "You're leaving, aren't you?" Concern and curiosity clashed in equal parts.

With his arguments ready, preparing for a small battle, he said, "Yes, in the morning." He watched as she nodded and then carefully picked his way ahead. "Jeff is staying behind to lead the team here at the house."

"Where are you going?" she asked, her gaze lowered to the quilt.

"The FBI sent orders requesting my presence at the Valley Forge reenactment."

"Why Valley Forge?" Being familiar with the area, she didn't see the connection.

"They're switching things up. It's smart on their part. No Civil War references. They have a reenactment from the War of Independence. The robbery ring's major players are meeting with the Copperheads to move some stolen artifacts. I found some information in one of my cyber-sweeps."

Pushing himself these last few days showed how much more was possible with his unique talent. And how much stronger he became when using them. The distance traveling from the out-of-body projection–riding data links–had increased. Astronomically.

The bio-digital interface now supports multiple data streaming connections simultaneously, a significant improvement from its previous limitation to just a single connection. The experience of multiple interfacing was truly spectacular, with the immersion in such intense energy feeling even more addictive than before. But Will would worry about that issue another day after the enemy was defeated.

Currently, repeatedly covering great distances has proven

crucial in staying ahead of this threat. And by traveling in so many directions, gathering intelligence, he could bait the trap perfectly. It was time to put some of that information to good use. Even though nothing came up in any of Will's cyber sweeps about James Patterson, it didn't mean those two Sons of Liberty agents wouldn't say anything about their interactions. And they were operating on borrowed time before a decision came down from Frank Marshall to pull James off his undercover mission.

Everyone in their group knew how protective Frank Marshall was of the people that worked for him. Add in the fact that James' wife, Lia, was the Associate Deputy Director's adopted daughter, and it wasn't hard to see why Frank would move to intervene in any situation that compromised James' safety.

"Are you going as part of the investigation team?" Allison's gaze leveled on her husband's chest, working hard to keep the fear from taking over.

"Kind of," Will replied, not elaborating.

"I see," Allison commented. However, by her facial expression, she looked anything but sure. "Can you tell me what has set this in motion?"

"Nothing other than the information about the reenactment. We're no closer to locating where the Sons of Liberty and Copperheads operate than we were before. Or determining their key players. We need to make a move to shake things up.”

“Why?” she questioned.

“So, we can end this once and for all!” Guilt had him losing the short leash on his patience. As well as another lie added to his tab. Right there with the one about her uncle hiring his company to watch over her. Guilt and maybe some uncertainty made his temper flare.

Doesn't she want a life with me away from all of this? His sudden worry about misreading the situation made him wonder if Allison still thought this investigation linked their time together.

If so, she needs to be prepared for a change of plans. I want it all.

“Are high-ranking FBI agents among the-” Allison brought her hands up and made an air-quote gesture with her fingers while saying, “We?” She dropped her hands and continued, “In wanting the critical people out in the open?”

Will studied her with fierce intensity. “Why do you ask?”

Allison scooted up and sat cross-legged, facing him. The fact that he answered with a question didn't escape her notice. “Because Will, the pattern is changing abruptly.”

Will's focus became fixated on something beyond her right shoulder.

"From the start, everyone has been putting a lot of effort into keeping you behind the scenes. So, what's changed?" Watching as Will's expression remained closed, she sighed.

"Plus, in reading the files, the reports publicly recognize the ongoing smuggler's case with no hint of the more serious threat. It makes sense that they continue to lay low, allowing their informant to be meshed deeper within the organization you're really after. To flush them out without knowing the key people would be a mistake."

She paused to spread her hands before her, smoothing the wrinkles between the bedding, inadvertently distracting Will's attention.

"Sooo..." Allison studied his features, carefully trying to break into their internal connection, but he still held that impenetrable wall up against her. She sighed heavily again. "It would seem something has happened to want you out in the open like this. And why is Jeff staying behind? I know he's more than just the liaison between agencies. Since the team now knows the real reason this organization wants you is more than just Nancy's obsession. Jeff's protection is prudent."

Will was seriously impressed and frustrated with her deductive reasoning. Jeff had been spot on when recognizing Allison's proficiency in this investigational work.

"You're right, Ally, but I won't be the bait. I will use my

abilities and keep myself aware of all communications surrounding the operation. No one will know I am there. The agency will provide additional coverage for me with men Jeff personally trusts. If I can't be here with you and Sara, I want Jeff guarding you both."

A part of what he told her was a lie. And Will hoped and prayed this risk paid off.

Using his unique telepathic ability to link to the internet, Will left a false leak from the National Park's offices. This information placed Will on location, helping with the artifacts' sting.

He had also sent false replies from the FBI and CIA agencies, with strict orders that William Maxwell's presence remained guarded and behind the scenes during the reenactment. This move would bring the rats to the surface.

"Will, you told me that we are completely safe here. I'd rather Jeff be with you. Or better yet, let Jeff and I come with you."

"Absolutely. Not." Will clasped her one hand and kissed her fingers. "I won't be able to do my job to the best of my abilities if I'm worried about you. I know it's not logical or fair, but you are to stay here. And I feel better knowing Jeff is here with you and Sara for the same reason."

Completing a successfully baited trap–using Will as the cheese–the agencies would be one step closer to knowing all the players. And more importantly, which side they played on.

Will believed the risk of possible capture was worth the price.

If they have me, they might leave my wife and child alone.

Allison's shoulders collapsed with a drawn-out sigh. "Oh, then you're telling me you have enough information from the inside informant to wrap up this assignment?"

"Yes. We have enough information," Will lied.

Allison saw determination and something else in his facial expression she couldn't quite put her finger on. "How long will you be gone?"

"I don't know. But if all goes well, I see this ending very soon." Will prayed that when it was all over, and she learned of his deception, she would understand why–and forgive him.

"Okay," she whispered. The fear of losing him wanted to make her rush in and build walls to protect herself emotionally. Especially since a nagging feeling about her uncle stayed just beyond her reach. But Will's assurances that the "Buchanan Curse" wouldn't keep them apart held a stronger appeal.

So, instead of seeking distance, she sought to get closer. Carefully positioning herself on top of his sculpted body, she parted her legs to straddle his waist. Her soft curves pressed and slid along his solid chest.

Her exhale warmed his sensitive flesh. When Will began to move, her hands pressed firmly on his shoulders to stop him.

"No. I want to have my way with you." Kissing along his jaw, she bit his neck softly.

Lips slowly trailed down his chest. Her hands lightly combed through his chest hair near where her mouth teased.

Will's hands fisted tightly in the sheets. The need to possess her rode him hard. The teasing of sensitive skin over tense muscles with lightly scraping nails trailing behind her lips and tongue would be his undoing.

Allison's body burned with a fever. Her power over him became an addictive drug pumping through her veins, and the need for more equaled the same as pulling in the air for her lungs.

When the wet heat of her lips destroyed him with deliberate attention, he arched off the bed. Tightly gripping the bedpost, he kept from grabbing her and taking back control.

"Baby! It feels so good," Will called out before an animalistic groan escaped his lips, dragging Allison's body upward. A mindless compulsion that would likely leave bruising on her tender skin took him over. Rolling on top, he spread her thighs wider.

With their joining, they both cried out in pleasure.

His hands held firm, one cupping her face, the other behind her neck. Keeping her confined, he devoured her with his lips and tongue.

She reveled in the power of his response. Her hands traveled down his back, nails digging into the flesh of his butt, urging him to soar. With each hard, unrestrained stroke, she burned with the need to have all of him.

The sensations of shooting stars exploded inside her head, and pulsing waves of intense pleasure seemed to rip through every nerve ending in her body.

Will stiffened. His expression reflected pain, but he yelled out in ecstasy.

When Allison came back to awareness, Will's arms still held her tightly. Tucking her head into the curve of his neck, she nibbled on the erratic pulse below his heated skin. Then, sighing with contentment, she dropped off to sleep.

Intermittently, throughout the night, Will woke her to make love repeatedly. His lovemaking held an intensity with their separation drawing near. He didn't want to leave his family, but his love for them made it necessary.

It was an essential part of his makeup to protect people, and when it involved his loved ones, there were no boundaries he wouldn't cross to see them safe.

He wouldn't let the time they spent apart be in vain.

Even if Allison discovered his lies, she and Sara would be far from danger. And Will would do anything to keep the fight centered on him.

Chapter Seventeen

A wide yawn spread across Allison's face as she blinked open her eyes. Exhaustion made an early wake-up the next day impossible. She woke up to the bright early-afternoon sunlight flooding the room, which made her eyes hurt.

She reached toward Will's side of the bed and found it empty.

A sleepy recall of Will rousing her to say goodbye floated to the surface. "I love you," he had whispered while brushing a light kiss on her cheek. "I'll call you later."

Now, stumbling into the shower, she wondered if that had been his plan all along. Allison tilted her chin up slightly–the process of washing her hair slowed significantly.

Did he purposely tire me out to avoid having me awake when he left?

Sighing, she dropped her chin to fall on to her upper chest. The heat of the water coated her head and face before running down her body. Letting the spray setting soothe her mild aches, she wondered if there would ever be a time when her husband wasn't a step or two ahead of her.

Hands lifted and rested on the tile wall, and Allison leaned further into the pulsating shower spray. The water had to work its magic to revive a sleepy mind and tired body because a suspicion began to form in Allison's thoughts that her obstinate husband required help.

The inconsistencies in everyone's behavior began piling up quickly.

Hint number one became her late start. Allison discovered that orders had come down from Will that ensured Allison slept as long as possible. At first, Allison took that as having a considerate husband. After all, he did keep her up until all hours of the night.

But that didn't last long.

Once she came downstairs, the doubts began to surface with Rebecca's and Jeff's avoidance. When she did manage to corner them, long hesitations seemed to be the status quo when seeking clarifications about the upcoming reenactment. The strange looks passed between Rebecca and Jeff or the awkwardness of Will's agents left behind at the house wasn't a good sign either.

The final inkling came directly before Will's late afternoon phone call.

By the pool, Rebecca had done a terrific job distracting Sara and, at the same time, giving her mother a wide berth. Allison overheard Sara telling Rebecca about a dream she had had with a man who said was her great uncle. With all the fanciful adventures during this dream, Allison didn't immediately connect the dots with Senator Buchanan until Sara said something that resonated within her memory.

Tossing the beach ball toward Rebecca, Sara said, "His superpower is making dreams. And now that Mommy and Daddy are together, they have superpowers, too. They can destroy any bad guy that gets in the way. He said I didn't have to worry about the bad guys winning because I can learn to fly like Daddy."

Rebecca's gaze traveled across the pool to meet Allison's. Her head tilted to the side with a frown appearing across her mouth.

Allison stood up to interrupt her daughter.

Ask Will if it is true. Then, ask yourself, how would this be possible to dream of if you didn't know anything about it previously? Her body jolted with that resurfaced memory, and she took that first step toward her daughter.

But Pete, a Guardians, Inc. agent, called out, "Allison, Will's on hold for you." He pointed to the portable phone on the outdoor countertop against the exterior wall. "Push in the extension that is flashing red."

She absently nodded while her attention stayed on her daughter. Sara continued to tell Rebecca about the outrageous visitors that came in her dreams and made happy things appear.

"Mrs. Maxwell, Will is waiting on the line."

"Yes, of course," Allison replied while heading for the phone. She pressed the button indicated and rested the receiver against her ear and mouth. "Will?" Allison called.

"Hey, Ally, How's everything going at the house?" Will's voice sounded strained.

"Umm. Uh, okay, I guess," she said as the memory of those dream-like connections with her uncle clicked in place.

Oh, my word. Can my uncle communicate through dreams?

Her responses to Will's conversation happened on autopilot as she thought about everything her uncle said while visiting her while sleeping. She leaned against the outdoor kitchen cabinet. Her free hand grasped her hair and slid a loose fist along the length of the styled ponytail positioned high on her head.

It was only when Allison snapped back to the present did their stale conversation become noticeable. "How's the investigation going?" Allison asked.

"Nothing to report. I'm just working on Guardians, Inc.'s dealings right now," he replied.

The pile-on of more dodged conversations without

mentioning the investigation became unmistakable. The numerous changes in that taboo category became the ebb and flow of their dialogue. Only when Allison voiced the one thing, urged by her uncle in the last dream-like state, did the stale–seemingly one-sided conversation–come to an end.

"Did my uncle hire Guardians, Inc. for my sister's and my protection?"

"Ally…" Will sighed. Her name, spoken in a barely-there tone following a long hesitation, signaled his struggle, but whatever was going on, he didn't share.

Instead, with a regretful voice, he said, "I love you. We'll talk about it when I come home. Please kiss Sara for me." The call ended. Averting away from another of Rebecca's frowning expressions, Allison let the heavy sigh escape.

Will had returned to his earlier mode of operation–keeping her in the dark.

Plus, the sinking feeling that she had been communicating with her uncle in dreams began to ring true. All this time passed between them, and she never knew he had such a remarkable ability.

Yet another person who kept her clueless.

Allison became equally determined not to remain there much longer.

****

An hour later, after Sara confirmed from one of the investigation's photos that Senator Buchanan was the man who came to her daughter's dream, Allison urgently felt the need to talk to her uncle.

But Allison's calls to her uncle kept going to voicemail.

Picking up drinks and snacks from the kitchen, Sara and Allison headed back to the pool. On their way outside, Sara began to dance in place. "Mommy, I need to go to the bathroom."

A quick detour to the powder room had Allison waiting nearby for her very independent child to use the bathroom. Alone.

Knowing how long her daughter would hold out before calling for help with her bathing suit, which Allison figured was a long wait. She took one more chance to reach her uncle. But this time, she dialed her family estate's housekeeper instead.

The call was picked up on the second ring.

Once getting the pleasantries out of the way, she gave her reasons for calling. Mrs. Roberta Lisson, having good relations with the former young mistress of the house, assured her that she would have Senator Buchanan return Allison's call when he came home. But she also mentioned that the Senator gave notice that he would be out of town for several days.

"Oh, well, if he gets in touch with you, let me know." Allison quickly recited the cell phone number Will gave her to use.

"Sure, Ms. Buchanan. Not a problem. But make sure you come for a visit soon. I miss seeing you," Mrs. Lisson said pleasantly.

On the tip of Allison's tongue was to correct the housekeeper on her new last name, but the less one knew about recent events, the more Will and Sara would avoid her family troubles.

"Absolutely. You know how much I love your apple-cinnamon muffins. We'll sit down and have a long talk over coffee," Allison promised then disconnected the call.

Leaning against the wall, she heard fragments of Rebecca's and Jeff's strong words just down the hallway near the control room. Sounding very much like their other past disagreements, Allison took no mind to them at first.

Until Will's name was mentioned.

Then she didn't hesitate moving closer and positioning herself just outside the slightly open door.

"You should have gone with Will when you had the chance," Rebecca retorted.

"And you should mind your damn business," Jeff replied.

"I mind my business by following my orders, something you don't seem to be doing too well for yourself," Rebecca taunted him. "If you show up now, you may endanger him."

"The agency had no right to use him like this, and he's too

personally involved to think straight. The information I just received gives me plenty of reasons to postpone using Will as the bait until I get there with more of my men in place.

"And as your immediate superior, I'm ordering you to stand down and get the hell out of my way." Jeff's voice held none of his normal, playful banter.

Allison stormed inside with a tray full of ammunition and let loose her attack.

Chapter Eighteen

Every last juice box, fruit roll-up packet, and snack-size bag of pretzels on Allison's tray got flung at Jeff.

He failed to dodge the aimed missiles, distracted by the know-it-all-agent-from-hell. Some of the things grazed Jeff's forehead while others hit the most tender spot of his anatomy. Luck would have it that the more harmful items of the mix missed their targets by quite a lot.

Allison's hands rested on her hips, and her face tilted in a blatant challenge. "Okay, Agent Patterson, who gets to shoot him first?"

"Oh shit," Jeff muttered. He raised both his hands in the air. "Okay," he said, then sighed. "Both of you settle down." Quickly taking Allison's arm, he guided her to a chair and cautiously took the empty tray from her hand. "Where's Sara?" he softly asked.

"Bathroom," she answered absently. Her mind began racing. She couldn't shake the relentless fear that her loving

Will, might somehow become the catalyst for a tragic turn of events.

Jeff reached for the phone on the desk and pressed down on the extension button connecting him to the second-floor hallway. "Pete… yeah, something has come up. Can you watch Sara for a few minutes while I meet with Agent Patterson and Allison? She is in the downstairs bathroom near the kitchen. Okay, thanks-" He paused to listen to Pete's reply. "Yeah… I will when I can."

Hanging up the phone, he pivoted slowly to face them. He crossed his legs out in front of him while leaning on the edge of the desk. Frustrated, he rubbed his face before saying, "Let's get this over with."

"Where's Will?" Allison inquired, worried.

"He is in Valley Forge," Jeff quietly answered.

"So that wasn't a lie," she murmured.

"No, that was the truth." Jeff let out a deep exhale and continued to tell her everything.

After their sparring lesson last night, Jeff and Will got a conference call from one of the teams handling the artifacts investigation the other night. They had a lead for a contact showing up at the Valley Forge War of Independence's reenactment. By receiving the starting point of this intel, Will snagged some crucial information using his abilities and found ties to a Croatian terrorist group financially backing the Sons of Liberty organization.

It was the next big break in the case since Allison dropped that bombshell a couple days ago. Will was determined to shake the tree to see what else fell.

"My gut tells me these particular backers don't care about the Sons of Liberty's politics. But for whatever reason, they're helping them for the time being," Jeff explained before continuing.

"Thanks to you, Allison, we now know the real reason for Nancy's obsession. Will convinced the higher-ups that this opportunity was perfect and would not come around again. His argument of flushing out the major players seemed sound, and the team jumped at it.

"There is also a chance to shut down this external financial backer and be one step closer to finishing this terrorist threat close to home. One way or another, Will is determined to find and expose the key people in charge of these groups. He wants the threat over you and Sara eliminated."

Jeff held back mentioning the alternative plan–on the chance Will was captured.

"Won't they sense a trap, having Will suddenly available now?" Rebecca challenged.

"No. Since Allison had been correct regarding the Sons of Liberty's true motives with Will, they've probably been studying him for a while now. They would know Frank Marshall contracted Will's company to retrieve any stolen Civil War items and return them to their rightful owners. Besides, Nancy would have told them about Will's genuine interest in Civil War weaponry. Like the others, she'd been led to believe that Will's curiosity overcame his caution. Especially if Will felt confident in his company's men and the agency's ability to secure his, Allison and Sara's safety."

Jeff shot a quick glance at Allison, then rubbed his forehead several times. He took a deep breath, exhaling slowly. "Will also let it slip that time away from you worked to his advantage."

He met Allison's direct gaze and locked on before continuing. "Letting it leak out how angry he was about not knowing about Sara. He gave hints that things aren't going well with your, ahh... relationship."

"Ahh. Putting the top-shelf stuff on the trap, I see. But why involve Sara?" Allison jumped up from her seat and began pacing back and forth in front of the desk.

Jeff placed his body in Allison's path, blocking her next pass.

Jeff ran the inside palm of his hands up and down on her arms. "Listen to me." He cupped his hands around her shoulders and squeezed briefly. Knowing that a million-and-one bad scenarios were playing out in her head, Jeff spoke with conviction. "Sara will be heavily guarded. No one will get to her."

Jeff and Allison were so focused on each other that an odd yet fleeting expression on Rebecca's face was overlooked.

"The information of yours and Will's parental relations to Sara has a paper trail now. Remember, Allison. They have spies everywhere. Will decided that the risk was worth the exposure if it sets up the scenario of him being vulnerable for capture," Jeff explained.

Clear thinking became imperative, and that was impossible while panicking. Allison took a deep breath and slowly blew it out. "You know Nancy's going to want to grab him, right. And it will have nothing to do with the Sons of Liberty," she added.

"Yes." Jeff pulled his fingers through his hair. "Will's banking on that. Plus, we think one of the leaders of the Sons of Liberty organization will be there, too. Not only because of his involvement with Nancy but because his obsession with any Civil War artifacts won't allow him to do otherwise," he inserted.

"I still think it's fishy that they would go to this reenactment." Allison shook her head while trying to work out the missing piece to this intricate puzzle.

"They would have realized by now we'd swarm over anything that has to do with Civil War events," Rebecca reasoned.

Jeff nodded briefly before adding, "They have deals to make, and they thought we were none the wiser because the venue has changed. And so far, doing their thing out in the open, but among large groups of people seems to be working for them."

Allison tilted her head to the side. "Why didn't you go with him?" she asked.

"Will contacted my superiors. I got orders to stay behind to protect you and Sara."

Rebecca crossed her arms tight to her chest and asked, "So why are you just now willing to disobey a direct order and interfere?"

Jeff angled his lanky frame toward Rebecca. A part of him didn't want to give her the satisfaction of an answer, but he knew Allison needed the truth.

"I just received information from a source, leaving me with

significant doubts.

"Because Director Campbell, the head of the special division, has volunteered himself and his team to go with Will and the National Park Services. More suspicious are his recent promotions from an obscure branch department within the FBI to this major homeland security division. I've discovered they have all occurred in a fast-track manner that I now find questionable."

"You think he's a mole for the Sons of Liberty," Rebecca clarified.

Allison stopped pacing and looked at Rebecca and then at Jeff.

After discovering the truth, a question kept playing in loop through Allison's head. *How can I stop my stubborn, selfless, but arrogant husband from making the biggest mistake of his life?*

"You're going to Valley Forge to stop the trap," Rebecca concluded.

If Will didn't end up getting kidnapped by their enemies, Allison wanted to maim him and a few other people–like Nancy Johnson, Director Campbell, and maybe her husband–herself.

As Allison watched Jeff nod, her face reflected a steely, determined resolve. "I'm going with you," she announced.

Not surprised at all by Allison's statement, Jeff's breath still got caught. He had hoped to avoid this discussion at all costs. His fiercely determined expression mirrored Allison's. He placed his hands on her shoulders again and responded to her outrageous statement. "You're right, Allison. Will was wrong to go without me. And I was a Barney to let him go alone. But under no circumstance can I agree with you coming along. You have no formal training for this kind of thing. Not only would Will kill me, but he has too much on his mind right now to add worrying about your safety to the mix."

"That's what I'm counting on," Allison stated. "If Will thinks there is a slight chance that I can be in danger, he will back off with this until he makes sure I'm somewhere safe before proceeding. I'll add one more if that's not a good enough reason. If you leave me behind, you better be prepared to keep me under lock and key. Because I'll be the biggest pain in the ass you and your team have ever seen. You won't have enough manpower to stop me. Especially when I get Senator Buchanan involved."

"Okay," Jeff calmly said. It was the only thing to say when Allison stood before him, resembling an enraged demigoddess–ready to throw down lightning bolts.

"We're already moving your sister and her family up here. I handpicked the agents that we could trust to bring them without acquiring a tail. Once they're en route, we'll leave together and contact Will when we're in the air. That will keep him put until we can meet up."

"What about me?" Rebecca leaned against the door panel, folding her arms over her chest.

"I need you here," Jeff grudgingly admitted. "Sara is comfortable with you. With her Mom gone, she'll need you close until the rest of the family arrives." Jeff turned back to Allison. "Your family is scheduled to be here early tonight."

With Allison's surprised look, Jeff explained, "Will thought it would be easier for you to have them close by just in case-"

"Okay! Okay," Allison interrupted Jeff, not wanting to hear the rest. She shot a look toward Jeff, then switched to Agent Patterson. "Rebecca… can you come here for a moment?"

Rebecca moved closer to Allison. Catching whispers but nothing he could understand, Jeff tried to pierce their mental shields with his telepathic abilities, but to no avail.

Suddenly, his gorgeous nemesis spun around and sent him a wicked smirk. "Be right back," she said, looking at him smugly.

Jeff's gaze tracked her exit from the room. He swiveled back and spoke to Allison sternly. "We don't have time to set up for a bottom turn. What are you up to?"

"I just asked her to get something for me and bring it back."

"Okay. Then I will gather my things and meet you back here." If he hurried, he planned to leave without Allison.

Jeff motioned to leave but was force-stopped in his tracks by two things: One became the soft-spoken order for him to stop, and the next stood more shocking of the two.

A gun leveled outward, pointing straight at him.

Chapter Nineteen

Delaware City had a population of about 1,695 people at the last census and was positioned on the eastern terminus of the Chesapeake and Delaware Canal. Since that previous census, not much had changed in this small port town with the population, architecture, or popular visitor attractions.

That time continued to pass–almost unnoticed by the town's residents and bordering areas–did well for the Sons of Liberty's agenda. For them, the main selling feature was the access to Pea Patch Island's State Park.

This island, located in the mid-channel of the Delaware River, got its name after a ship full of peas ran aground, spilling its contents and leading to the plant's growth on the island. In addition to the historical features of the State Park, the wetlands provided a significant stop for migratory birds along the Atlantic Flyway.

During the War of 1812, the island became a defense Fort of New Castle, Delaware.

In 1831, a fire wrecked the original structure. Construction continued a few years later, creating a much larger polygonal layout. The Fort was fully completed in 1860 and used throughout the Civil War by the Union as a camp for Confederate prisoners.

Around the turn of the century, a large battery for three–then-modern–12-inch guns on a disappearing carriage was built in the Fort as part of the Endicott program. That machine marvel, back then, got joined with batteries for smaller guns elsewhere on the island. And just like the previous wars, this approximately one-mile-long island's location gave the Sons of Liberty an additional advantage.

But time took its toll, and like most things, the island aged with neglect.

When the Historical Restoration program finally added the Fort to its project list a couple of years ago, the Sons of Liberty swooped in and took over. They confiscated the island from under all the officials' noses in plain sight.

Under the guise of Engineers, Restoration specialists, and stuffy bureaucrats, the members of the Sons of Liberty and the Copperheads came and went without anyone the wiser.

And the man–with the all-black wardrobe–presently stepping off a sidewalk curb took the most advantage of this isolated refuge. As the crossing light flashed its consent, he eased through the intersection of Harbor Street and Clinton Street.

Mr. Black's attention rested on his ride, docked at the ferry terminal's pier. The public accessibility by Forts Ferry Crossing, from both the Delaware and New Jersey banks to Pea Patch Island, remained in operation and a favorite public attraction. But with the facility closed for repairs, only the renovation crew and restricted personnel could get access to and from the island.

Black's partner in crime–and overall personal shadow–stood stoically waiting for him with the small crew operating the double-tiered boat ready to push off.

Having gone ahead of his employer, once the light-gray Bentley Mulsanne–located two blocks away was parked–Michael prepared for their departure upon Black's arrival aboard the passenger's ramp. Allowing Mr. Black to stay behind to finish up a crucial call.

The unknown puppeteer hijacking these nefarious terrorist groups stood just within Black's reach. Shedding light on their hidden agenda would reveal the true scope of their madness. Only time would tell if a specific FBI agent got entangled in this organization's madness. This, among other things, made Mr. Black's current lateness a more than fair exchange.

With a discernible jerk of his chin, Mr. Black signaled to Michael.

His trusty companion turned away and immediately set things in motion with the crew.

The familiar noise from the terminal's activity blended with the seagulls flying around, looking for food near the waterfront. Mr. Black became mindful of rearranging priorities after today's call.

Unfortunately, with Michael Arenald's focus divided–to order the ferry lines casting off from the terminal–it took the attention off his employer. Or Black's chauffeur would have shouted out in warning.

As Mr. Black stepped away from the curb, past one from among several parked cars within the ferry's parking lot, a throttling roar came out of nowhere, aiming directly for him.

A push came from behind, shoving him toward the on-coming pick-up truck.

He cursed silently at himself. The carelessness of not staying aware of his surroundings would be his present downfall. And the grievously bad timing would put a kink in their mission, especially when this organization could finally reveal the secrets of Black's nefarious past.

Because, as everyone knew, once you could see something, you could study it.

And then dissect it.

But more importantly, in Mr. Black's case, he could destroy

it.

Just before he felt the deathly impact of metal mass combined with an accelerated momentum, a forceful tackle got him clear of the hit-and-run attempt. Slamming the ground hard, he and his rescuer rolled a few yards away, landing close to the opposite side of the parking lot.

Miles Jenning's harsh whisper, "Get up, boss. Move!" Got Black up and dashed to the safety of the nearest parked car. His savior followed him close behind.

Thinking they were in the clear came a second too soon.

Several pings nearby notified them of a sniper in their vicinity. Black's agent took offense to the additional attack as a slew of Cockney-influenced swearing words spilled out under his breath. Miles' gaze briefly mourned his favorite Walkman as it was exhibited in a fragmented mess on the asphalt of the parking lot's surface.

Deadly shots sprayed downward around them, keeping them pinned to the area. At the same time, the partner of the hit-and-run perpetrator jumped inside the passenger's side of the truck, and they both peeled away between skidding rubber and a commotion of the nearest ferry's personnel shouting at their retreating rear end.

MJ met Black's piercing, glinting eyes. The regular neutral expression on his employer's face was long gone. In its place stood a chilling ire that Miles hoped was directed at their enemy, and not him.

"Boss, you got to make a break for it. The terminal's outbuilding should give you some protection. I'll lay down some cover."

The direction of the bullets' trajectory gave away the shooter's spot. Knowing what to look for, MJ focused on the minuscule reflection, pinpointing the sniper's exact location.

A high tower at Emmanuel Presbyterian Church stood two blocks away. MJ's marksmanship was impressive, but the sun's position gave their attacker the advantage.

However, Miles just needed to provide the shooter with something to worry about.

Taking aim, using the nearby car's hood as a steading base, he shouted, "Go now!" His fired shots centered around the tower's bell opening, facing the port side. He heard rather than saw his employer sprint away.

Two shots followed Black's retreat, but the shower of bullets MJ sent in the general direction of the attacker worked well as a distraction. The sniper's aim had gone berserk.

Miles fired off several more rounds before he took his advice and made for a safer cover. His dash across the small grass area separating the lot and the pavement just before the Ferry Terminal's outbuilding took the shooter by surprise.

He made it to the side of the ticket office and turned the corner toward the waterside when his body jolted with the bullet's impact.

Michael Arenald had swung around the opposite side of the terminal, along the pier on the waterside. It took him several shots before their sniper got hit and fell from the church's bell tower opening. With the threat eliminated, he hurried along the building's back exterior face until he came to the small huddle of bodies surrounding a downed man.

Coming up to the body, he spotted Mr. Black and pressed two fingers on the man's pulse point on the neck.

His gaze raised and met Michaels.' A list of calmly stated commands was given without missing a beat, "Okay. Hudson, call our contact at Delaware City and get this incident brushed aside. Everyone else, get back to work."

Mr. Black rose from kneeling and gestured for Michael to come closer. His voice came out in a sharp but low-volume reprimand. "He'll be sore but fine. His bullet-proof vest took most of the hit."

A quick scan of the surrounding area did little to reconcile how many potential witnesses saw what had happened. That would be a problem for another day.

"What's the deal with MJ being out in the open? I had left standing orders stating he was to remain hidden away."

The chauffeur's head tilted to the side, switching his attention back to the unconscious man, Arenald's new partner. A forced partnership that neither man had wanted but was proving to be an effective mix.

Before Michael gave a reply, a deeply burden-upon sigh escaped. The seriousness of the circumstances made his strong posh accent even more clipped than usual. "Well, Sir, in all fairness. If MJ had... listened, you would be on the ground in his place. Would you not?"

His displeasure of Black putting himself in this situation in the first place came across with a glaring stare down and a clenching jaw. "And let's not forget. Setting his protective vest's positive outcome aside, you can't come back from the dead as well as our associate here."

Black gave a heavy sigh, perfectly matching his counterpart's in tone, volume, and spanning length. He looked around at the few men, who still kept their attention centered on them, and his demeanor went even stiffer.

When his cold gaze trailed along each and every one of those men and caught their attention, one by one, they soon found something else to keep them occupied.

"Come on," Mr. Black softly ordered. "Help me get him on the boat. We'll let him recuperate on the ride over to Pea Patch's Fort. You two can take the boat back after dropping me off."

Chapter Twenty

"What?" Jeff yelled with a few explicated curses about the conniving nature of women.

"Jeff… don't worry. It's just Rebecca's taser gun. You're Will's best friend. I could never hold a real gun on you," Allison assured him calmly, shifting her stance to a more secure footing.

"Although, if you take one step toward that door or call out, I have no qualms about shooting you on a low setting at a sensitive part of your anatomy. More than one time." Allison directed her gaze downward to the area between his legs. "I don't want to do that because your recoup time will mess up the schedule."

Jeff winced and moved his hand to cover his male member.

Allison grinned and added, "There are things I need, and I don't want to risk you leaving without me. Your capitulation went way too easily."

Damn it! Jeff mentally cursed Allison's suspicious nature. And the fact that she was correct in her thinking didn't help.

"And how do you plan on accomplishing anything while keeping a gun on me?" he asked with a superior smugness that Allison believed must be a typical trait of an FBI agent.

"That's simple." Allison shrugged and added, "Rebecca."

Jeff looked utterly flabbergasted and then quickly overtaken by outrage. "We don't have time for this, Allison! I promise you. I'm not planning on leaving without you."

Well, not now... Jeff admitted silently.

"I'm not leaving you until we are on that plane and in the air." Allison nodded once in conclusion to that promise.

His telekinesis ability could take care of that gun in a heartbeat. But he didn't want to hurt Allison and take the chance of the gun going off by accident. Allison's words and body language held such conviction it would be a waste of time to dispute anyway. She'd find a way to follow him and risk having no backup protection. At least this way, he could keep her safe.

He gave in with a loud groan. "You know, you really should reconsider a career change. You'd make a pretty good field agent," he grumbled.

****

Sitting in the cockpit of yet another small plane a few moments later, Jeff got some well-deserved payback for Allison's obvious discomfort.

In reality, calling it discomfort was putting it mildly. The co-pilot's seatbelt strapped her in so tight he wondered if she could take a full breath.

"Are we ready to go?" She spoke, like someone heading to their execution.

"Just about. A few more items on the final pre-flight checklist, and we'll take off." Seeing her like this took the edge off some of his frustration. "Look, Allison, sit in the back; it may be easier."

"No. I still don't trust you not to try something." Pete and Mike escorted them, with haste, to this neighboring property on golf carts used for ground maintenance. They loaded all the supplies onto the two buggies and stored them quickly inside the plane. She still couldn't believe they allowed her to board without trying anything.

"Plus, I need to get past this-" Allison waved her hand, encompassing the cockpit's controls. Outside the front window, the normal activity surrounding the large equestrian farm carried on, as if having their small jet parked off to the side was a regular occurrence.

Jeff continued checking the instruments, flipping switches, and adjusting controls. The engine revved, the plane maneuvered toward the runway and began to increase speed.

Only after the jet engine's acceleration sounds diminished and their position leveled off could he hear a small exhale released from Allison. Jeff reached over and adjusted the fasteners so her next breath came more freely.

His grin turned lopsided, watching her clasp the buckle's adjustment tightly in her hand afterward. Like she considered rectifying the harnesses' roomier hold the first chance she got.

"Okay, co-pilot, we have a little under two hours in the air. Let's go over some of the instruments before we land."

The more knowledge she gained about the aircraft's abilities, the less chance fear could take over her mind. The plushness of light tan, leather seats, gleaming, off-white colored fiberglass, and cherry wood interior took little notice over the array of gears, glass displays, gauges, and wide bowed, tempered glass console.

But once the mind grasped that they remained in one piece and still moving through the air, she managed to take in the splendor beyond the windshield. With the sun beginning to set, a vast blue sky had hints of pink, purple, and pale orange hues around the clouds.

Her hand reached over and grabbed onto Jeff's to squeeze on tight. This time, it wasn't due to a gripping, petrifying fear that caught her breath, but instead, the astonishment of witnessing a living watercolor of blending colors surrounding them as they flew through the sky.

The beauty around her eased away some of her worries for

a short moment.

Too bad it didn't last for long. The fear of being too late to get to Will returned as soon as the light faded from the view.

She knew Will didn't believe in curses. But Allison wondered if he could make it any easier to tempt fate.

A half-hour out from landing, after blocking numerous telepathic attempts from Will, Jeff reopened their internal link and sent a quick message: *Get to a secure location and be ready for my call.*

Jeff immediately got a frustrated response back. *You better be quick about it.*

When Jeff hit the speed dial button, Will picked up on the first ring. "Where the fuck are you?" Will asked abruptly before adding, "I can't reach Allison."

"I'm close to a private landing site, and your wife is with me." Jeff omitted the fact that Allison practically forced her hand in the matter.

"You had better have an excellent reason," Will spoke with a deadly intensity.

"Oh, brah, don't get choppy. You need to hold off on setting yourself up as bait until we can talk." Jeff caught Allison's wild hand, gesturing off to the side. "Here's Allison." He handed over his satellite phone and began verifying his flight coordinates to prepare for the descent.

"Will, don't even think about doing anything stupid."

"I may put you over my knee when I get my hands on you. You're putting yourself in danger with this latest stunt, Allison!"

"Look who's talking! I'm not currently setting myself up as bait," she countered.

"It's not like that. Everything is checked and secured."

"No, it's not. Just promise me you won't set up anything until we talk. You owe me, Will. For keeping secrets about my uncle. Just wait, okay?"

"Fuck!" Will muttered.

"Tell him not to let anyone know we talked," Jeff mentioned.

She repeated Jeff's direction and added, "We'll call you when we land in about-"

"Thirty minutes," Jeff confirmed.

"Jeff says, thirty minutes. Be safe." Allison hung up and held tight to the phone. She stole a look at Jeff, sighing heavily. "Do you think he will listen?" she asked.

"Yeah, you were right earlier. He won't risk anything if you're in the open, too."

Allison nodded before adding, "Where are we meeting up?"

"A secure place outside the Valley Forge area that no one else knows about–except Will."

Jeff's gaze narrowed on Allison's palms, pressing into the fabric of her pants numerous times. Anticipating the need for a distraction, he cocked his head to the side and shot her a mischievous grin. "Okay. I need your help with the landing checklist. To add to your flying lesson."

"Keep dreaming," Allison retorted as her hands stilled.

A snicker escaped Jeff's lips. With his intent clearly on track, he began giving step-by-step orders as they went through the touch-down routine.

The landing went smoother than any other Allison had recalled. For once, the fear of crashing was low on her list of concerns. Jeff's mixture of tough love with clear, precise explanations gave her the determination to reduce the mindless panic to a resigning discomfort.

Allison may never enjoy flying, but she could learn to tolerate it.

Shutting down the engine, Jeff told her to stay put as he

moved out of the cockpit.

No sounds drifted back to her location, so she kept her eyes on everything outside the cockpit window. Unfortunately, whatever Jeff was up to happened beyond her view. Her hands rubbed a path along her thighs as she bit down hard on her lower lip.

Unlocking the T-hangar door, Jeff pushed the single door aside. Near the center structural post, he went inside, where a mechanical wenching box was mounted halfway up the metal column. Switching to the manual release, he pulled the hook and attached a cable from the T-hangar winch to the aircraft's tail end.

When the aircraft cleared the entrance's threshold, he shut down the winch, unhooked the cable from the tail end, and secured the fasteners away.

Shortly afterward, he joined Allison in the cockpit and went through the rest of the shutdown procedures.

Noticing her nervousness as she fidgeted with the unfastened seatbelt and the adjustable armrest, he gave her something to do. "Please go and offload our stuff from the luggage compartment. Leave it outside near the exit. I'll finish up here and join you. We need to move fast."

Nodding in acknowledgment, she took a long, calming

breath before jumping out of her seat.

"You did good, Ally," Jeff said while grinning. "I'll make a pilot out of you yet."

"Bite your tongue–and don't call me Ally!"

Jeff's chuckle landed him a playful smack on his head as she went out. "Do you want me to call Will now?" she asked, gathering the smaller bags from the cabin's lounge area.

"No, after we unload our gear," he instructed.

"Where are we unloading?" Allison asked, not having seen anything during their landing, having centered all her concentration on the controls and Jeff's instructions.

"Around back."

With one satchel on each shoulder and miscellaneous canvas bags in each hand, Allison made her way from the interior luggage compartment to the bottom of the aircraft steps. As her lungs graciously inhaled a full breath and quickly exhaled, a realization came to the forefront of her thoughts. Managing fabric books, furniture binders, and other interior samples had become the norm for her working with Debbie and Jake.

Her gaze took in the array of sizes and textures of the satchels and duffle bags as she dumped everything on the concrete floor near the plane.

How far all this was from her daily life would be an understatement; even if this moment seemed like deja vu from her time at work with her friends. And as Sara's favorite movie line goes, 'Lions, Tigers, and Bears. Oh, my' was never as relatable to her as right this minute.

Allison prayed things worked out better for herself and her companions than what happened to Dorthy and her crew after meeting the Wizard.

Chapter Twenty-One

A hand grabbed her shoulder while her name was called out. "Allison?"

She jolted and stepped back, causing Jeff's hand to drop. He started to move closer, but she put her hand out to stop him. "You know..." Her throat tightly constricted. She coughed and swallowed several times before continuing, "I've lost people I loved to threats I didn't understand."

She turned away and dropped her gaze to her clenched hands pressed to her stomach. "My uncle told me that being a Buchanan came with a price. One, that... he said I could mitigate if I took certain precautions. And I've tried to do just that. But I've done it my way, not his."

Jeff gently turned her around to face him. "I understand. I have burdens to carry due to my family, too. But-"

"No, Jeff. Let me say this," Allison urged in a rushing plea while sweeping her hand toward the bags on the ground. "I hid away from my family's obligations, not wanting my uncle's way of life. He gave me an out, and I grabbed it with both hands. When taking that job at JSB3, the only load I had to carry were the frivolous samples for projects and disappointing my clients.

"My friendship with Debbie and Jake is the only worthy outcome of hiding myself these last few years. And to make matters worse, I chose to keep that relationship at a comfortable distance. Using the Buchanan curse as the excuse to do it," she rebuked and sighed before continuing, "I'm hardly making a big difference or any difference for that matter in the world."

"From what I know of Debbie and Jake's clients, JSB3 has created some great projects. Worthy works of architecture and interior spaces that provide functional areas for many good people."

"Yes, I know," Allison agreed softly. "But I didn't work on those ventures. Having my involvement in those projects would have brought unwanted complications. Press and bureaucrats want a tit-for-tat to start with. I brought in the clients who wanted the right to claim that Allison Buchanan did their kitchen or bedroom suite," she scoffed.

"Those spaces are just as important. Life is hard, Allison. What you do provides an oasis from the harsh realities of living. Calling a place home is more than just giving walls to a house," Jeff argued.

Allison shrugged her shoulders, not believing him. "I see now that I kept myself insulated from feeling any loss. Like what I felt when my father died and, years later, my mom and stepdad. Plus, losing my sister after they died made it worse."

"Why didn't you and your sister stay together?" Jeff asked. His curiosity couldn't stop the words from escaping. He had reviewed her files when the Sons of Liberty put her in their crosshairs.

"Because my uncle told me it would be safer for Peggy. So, she went with my step-father's family, and I didn't fight it when Senator Buchanan was awarded my guardianship. My mother's legal will allowed me the power to choose," she told him.

Her voice dropped to a whisper, adding, "I didn't even fight for Sara. Gosh, I'm ashamed. It was easier letting Peggy and Bob assume the role of Sara's parents, allowing me to be the fun Auntie."

"I don't believe that," Jeff said while grabbing her hand. "Being Senator Buchanan's niece is no picnic. And I'm sure as the role of his ward, it wasn't any easier. Your family has many enemies. You didn't want that for Sara." Jeff gave a slight squeeze on Allison's hand before continuing. "I've had numerous conversations with your uncle, and he is not easy person to say no to. Can you imagine what Sara's life would have been like?"

"True. But he has his reasons for being that way," Allison interjected. "He's lost a lot of people close to him, too. It was tough for him to give me some breathing room."

She blew out a loud exhale. "Although it seems even that was an illusion." Curiosity got the best of her when she asked, "Did you know about my uncle hiring Will's firm to provide protection after we broke up?"

Jeff held his hands up, palms facing outward. "That is between you and Will. I plead the fifth."

Allison shrugged and turned away. "Anyway, what I was trying to articulate earlier is that this experience has done me some good, although it comes with some terrible aspects. It has opened my eyes.

"My whole existence had been a big shame-"

"You are being too hard on yourself, Ally- Uh, Allison," Jeff added.

"No. I'm not," she swiftly disagreed. "I took the easy path."

The Senator's message became clear to her. The path taken alone was no longer an option. She needed to make a stand.

Being part of a friendship, a family, and a team made sense. Fear was the only thing holding her back.

"I know I can do much more than I've done in the past, regardless of whether or not the Buchanan curse is real…

"I'm done hiding behind it," Allison vowed.

****

In City Point, Virginia, Mr. Sharpe's efficient assistant picked up a call before it rang twice. "Mr. Sharpe's office. Yes, Sir. I'll see if he is available. Hold, please." Placing the caller on hold, Jennifer Daniels pressed the intercom extension. "Sir, Director Cam- I mean, Mr. Green is on hold on line one for you. Would you like to take the call or have me take a message?"

"I'll take his call." He disconnected the intercom, and she watched as the blinking light on her phone display switched to solid. While completing her project, she kept an eye on the open line. The call lasted just short of six minutes before finishing. Immediately after, the intercom extension buzzed, and she pushed the button to connect them. "Yes, Sir?"

"Daniels. Go. Whatever you didn't complete, you can finish up in the morning."

"Sir, as requested, I'll visit the Freedman's site tomorrow to meet with Andrew McKnight."

"That's right. You can take the file with you and finish it there in the morning. I'll expect it around zero-nine-hundred." (9:00 a.m.)

Edward Sharpe hung up, and Jennifer began closing out the file marked for completion before leaving for the night. She copied it to her USB drive. Noticing the phone line light up again, she opened the bottom drawer, pretending to struggle with her cumbersome bag while switching to voicemail for the night.

Quickly clicking on another device behind a false file divider, she locked her desk and computer. Her desk area got thrown into the shadows as the fixture on her desk clicked off. The old air conditioning compressor filled her ears while following her normal routine of closing down for the day.

Her suspicions about Sharpe's growing snugness could not bode well for her team's cause. A cause that directly opposed the Sons of Liberty and Copperheads. And like herself, Sharpe did well with hiding his true motives away from prying and unwanted eyes.

She strained to overhear the conversation in the adjacent room, but it was useless. Leaving only one overhead light on, she strolled out of the office and headed to her private room.

Sitting at his desk, Sharpe pulled out the files regarding the

Maxwell family while getting a quick update from Campbell. After the call ended, another number was immediately dialed. He wasted no time with the pleasantries when the line was open–though he would have liked to linger.

"Nancy, get everything ready for tomorrow's exchange. I want that artifact collected no matter what. I don't care what else is going on. We're making a bundle selling those stupid items to our buyer." Sharpe paused, listening intently to what Nancy had to add. When she made her point, he nodded while saying, "Make it look good and call your contact to arrange for Mr. Maxwell's pick up. Yes. I want him at the Freedman's Village facility. Call me when it is done."

He disconnected and immediately dialed another number. While placing his call on speakerphone, he walked the length of his office, opened the connecting door, and cautiously looked around.

A single overhead light remained on. It did little good other than showing the clearances around the larger objects in the space and locate the exit door. Dark shadows lingered around all the niches and corners of the room.

Sharpe flipped the toggle switch that flooded the room with more light. After finding the office empty, he softly closed his door as the call was connected.

"Senator Buchanan speaking."

"Senator, we need your assistance in a small matter concerning your niece, Allison Maxwell."

"Of course, Mr. Sharpe…"

Chapter Twenty-Two

Jeff patted Allison's arm once before returning to the aircraft. He lifted the steps, tucked the folding stairs inside, and secured the door.

The hangar lay thick in the darkness with the sun's setting and the plane's interior lighting absent; only the dim illumination from the outside lights projecting through scattered windows kept them from complete blackness.

Reaching into one of the bags and finding the flashlights, Jeff gave one to Allison. Seeing the fear reflected in her eyes, he quickly smiled and gave his reassurance. "We're safe here." Pointing toward how they came in, he said, "Go close the door."

While following his directions, she checked out the surroundings.

The night hung with moist heat and complete stillness that seemed unnatural. No crickets or frogs chirped. No traffic sounds came near them. Her glance around only confirmed that earlier impression; there was no hint of civilization by sound or lights in the distance.

Only a barren runway was visible. The few exterior fluorescent lights on long poles illuminated only emptiness. As the corrugated metal panel slid closed, the scraping sound made Allison's ears hurt. With the door shut, she lost a major channel to the exterior lights, and the flashlight beam became her only friend through the murky void.

Heading to the bags left behind, she picked up one of the large canvas satchels and hugged it close to her chest. That quick look around outside showed no cover to hide behind other than this one building, so her nervousness prevailed even after Jeff's assurances. As Jeff called her name, the bag jerked in her hand, nearly slipping from her grasp.

"Ally, come around to the locker room. Let's get changed real quick."

"Stop calling me Ally!" she hissed back while hurriedly picking up the smaller bags that held the items needed. Using a dome of illumination seemingly dancing in the shadowed interior as a beacon, she met up with Jeff in the only room within the expansive hangar near the back.

His flashlight's beam skimmed along the rear perimeter of the hangar until it highlighted a package lying on the floor. Checking the door to the pilot's locker and office, Jeff gestured for her to go ahead when finding it open.

While he leaned down to pick up the medium-sized box,

Allison must have found the toggle switch for the room's fluorescent fixtures. A bright blue illumination spilled out from the door's opening as he followed her inside. He laid the box on a transaction shelf at the front reception desk.

He reached into his back pocket and pulled out a Swiss Army knife, placing it beside the package.

His two loud taps on the laminate counter successfully centered Allison's attention on the waiting box.

Reaching for his cell phone and pushing the speed dial button, Jeff tapped the speaker button and set the phone beside Allison.

"Maxwell," Will answered on the first ring.

"We're heading to the townhouse. Can you get there tonight?" Jeff asked.

"I can be there in under forty-five minutes. I have some of my security people here, so Director Campbell is relaxed with officially assigning me agents. I don't think I got shadowed."

"Copy." Jeff looked at his watch. "Let's say twenty-forty-five (8:45 p.m.)–out." Jeff hit the button to disconnect and looked toward Allison. "Open the box."

Jeff handed Allison his pocketknife. She split open the top and flipped over two sides. Moving the stiff brown packing paper out of the way, she pulled out two rubber-banded bundles of twenty-dollar bills, three cell phones, and a handgun with ammunition.

"One of the phones is for you. Speed dial numbers are already programmed. If we get separated, I want you to contact the two numbers at the end. Okay?"

"Yes." Allison put the phone aside and placed the other items on the length of the reception countertop. She maneuvered the empty box to the tall, rectangular, plastic trashcan beside the desk.

"Get yourself used to the phone. Look at the list and tell me if you have any questions." Jeff glanced at her, taking his attention off one of the satchels he was rummaging through.

Picking up the phone, it illuminated with a lock screen.

"Code is two, thirty-five, ten," he instructed while pulling several small containers out to lay next to the stack of money. "I'll get changed first while you check out the phone." After grabbing his bag, he left.

As she familiarized herself with its features, Jeff could be heard moving around in the adjoining room. His movements echoed loudly in the unnaturally still surroundings, like a confined elephant jostling within a cramped stall.

Locating the address book, she scrolled down the list. Will's number was on top, followed by Jeff, Rebecca, Pete, Jake, Peg, and two unknown contacts.

"Who are Shadow and Cutter?" She raised the volume of her

voice to carry over the racket Jeff made nearby.

"They're agents I trust. If we get separated, call them. They're close and on standby."

"Got it," Allison said and continued to review the phone. Knowing Jeff was right about preparing in case of an emergency, she didn't rush through all the features.

Several minutes later, looking up at the sound of Jeff's approach, Allison let out a snicker at his transformation.

The soft tread of Jeff's approaching figure negated what you'd expect to hear when seeing his visual appearance. His jeans molded his lean frame, giving the impression of more height, but the scuffed-up black leather jacket with red sleeves covering the equally scuffed-up T-shirt brought the whole look together. The heavy, full-length street boots with chains wrapping at the bottom certainly made a statement and explained the earlier noises coming out of the room.

Although he wore it well, Allison didn't believe the objective of blending in and going unnoticed was being accomplished. The man standing nearby reminded her of a blonde version of the Wolverine character from the X-Men comic book–without the facial hair. His beach bum persona was long gone, and she suspected this look came closer to the real him than the other.

"Wow!" Allison fanned her face and gave a soft, smoldering whistle.

Jeff grinned wickedly, leaning against the desk. "You mistakenly married Will when this was available to you." Gesturing along his body, he extruded an arrogant sexiness that would raise any woman's temperature.

But Allison's remained steady. Only one man got her flushed and bothered, and it wasn't Jeff. "Well. Okay then." She snorted. "Can you get over yourself now?"

"I can if you can." He grinned before a more serious look took over his demeanor.

"Okay, your turn. I'll load up our things while you get your disguise on." Jeff took the stack of money, gun, ammunition, and the other cell phone off the counter and stuffed them in his now partially empty leather satchel. His gaze trailed from the duffle bag near her foot up to her eyes. He tilted his chin toward the room he came from and said, "Call out when you're done changing."

Allison watched as he stuffed a rubber door stopper under the office door to keep the panel fully open. The encroaching darkness beyond the room's illumination gradually swallowed him as he moved farther away.

All that remained was a discombobulated floating cone-shaped glow of his flashlight. Then, even that disappeared as he cut around the exit and got lost from her view.

A prayer got sent out into the universe as the shadows

around her began to feel foreboding.

Please don't let my husband do anything stupid before we get there.

****

Nancy Johnson hurried down the steps from the high-rise apartment complex in the center of Washington, DC.

The call she had hoped to get had just set things in motion.

Her hands raised to fluff up her hair, and the long locks settled effectively around her face. The dark, power-red shade she usually wore was changed to a rich chestnut color. The exact tone and auburn-colored highlights, reflected in all of the recent photos of Allison Buchanan-Maxwell, were duplicated at the fancy salon she just exited.

Moreover, it cost a bundle for the service. A service that was only extended to a selected clientele. Very selective clientele.

"But so worth every penny," she said softly. Nothing could subdue the dark blue eyes that glittered with excitement. Her patience was finally being rewarded. By Nancy's calculations, Will Maxwell will be in the Copperhead's grasp soon; and his sorry excuse of a partner would have no chance of stopping it.

Coming to a stop at the bottom landing of the parking lot's stairway, she grabbed the cell phone tucked in the back pocket of her skin-tight jeans. A cold smile slowly set in place when dialing a number by memory.

Storing any preset numbers was definitely not an option when dealing with the group of people she associated with these days. She had multiple burner phones to ensure her calls stayed under the radar.

When the caller picked up, she had no time for pleasantries. "I'm heading your way. Make the call at the agreed time, and I'll see you there within the next hour." The night's cool air brushed against her face as she pushed open the exit doors and moved the soft, wavy curls around her head and shoulders. The light, auburn shades of her new hairdo gleamed under the nearby streetlamps and softened the sharp features of her face.

But nothing could soften the blaring obsession that drummed through her bloodstream.

Will Maxwell would be mine by tomorrow morning.

Chapter Twenty-Three

Allison picked up her bag from the New Garden's airplane hangar in Chester County, Pennsylvania, then shuffled into the adjacent locker area.

A small sink and toilet took one side of the room, while a row of two-tiered lockers divided an open shower area with several showerheads spaced a couple of feet apart. The room appeared much bigger from what you could determine from the office side.

Spotting the small bench against the nearby wall, Allison sat down and kicked off her sneakers and capris. She changed into Levi's Matchstick jeans with fraying seams and worn holes in the knee areas. A short-sleeve T-shirt with a skull and crossbones logo went over her long-sleeved white cotton shirt. The mid-calf, scuffed-up street boots finished off the look and felt utterly alien to her.

"I'm decent. Well, kinda," Allison called out into the darkness, making her way to the front reception desk.

"Noted," Jeff yelled, his voice echoing from the hangar out

back. He sounded close but not within the boundaries of the outward shining light spilling from the office's open door.

Allison held a fistful of denim to keep them up as she bent down to gather up her discarded clothes and stuffed them back into the knapsack. She grabbed the phone from the counter and stuffed it in her front pocket. Then she jammed her handbag into the remaining satchel.

A very unladylike snort escaped Allison's mouth before adding, "I don't think my disguise is equally convincing as yours. My pants are going to fall off."

Jeff laughed while stepping into the room. A folded green tarp lay tucked beneath his armpit as he wrapped a bungee cord around his hand in a loose bundle. "Here's something to help you." Handing the bungee cord to Allison, he reached for the larger container on the transaction counter. Opening it up, he took out a dark leather shaving kit that sat inside with a few other odds and ends.

After gesturing for Allison to come closer, he opened the bag and peeled off a Mustache Goatee from its paper backing. His gentle pat on her chin and upper lip set the fake, stylized beard in place. Leaning back to examine, he nodded. "I think that helps a little; let's do something with your hair. Pull it into a low ponytail."

While Allison followed his suggestion, Jeff rummaged

through the remaining saddlebag and pulled out a red bandana. Folding it into a large triangle, he wrapped it around her hair and secured it tight from the back.

"There you go. Now, about those pants. Give me the cord." Jeff motioned to the bungee cord she still held. She handed it back to him, and he threaded it through the loops of her jeans and fastened the hooks in the front. "How's that feel?"

Letting go of the fist of fabric, she tested the effectiveness. "Good," Allison noted.

"With your helmet on, the overall disguise will work even better." Jeff's present goal of not wanting to leave anything behind caused him to miss Allison's wide-open mouth frozen in place.

"Okay. Help me load the last of this stuff on the bike," he said while searching the surrounding surfaces.

A quick throw of one of the smaller bags to Allison got her mouth to close. Her body jerked in motion as she caught the tossed item while juggling the one she already had in her grasp.

Jeff's abrupt exit prompted her to follow. They made their way to the exterior door with large and hurried strides.

Allison stumbled on the uneven ground. The darkness hit her like a solid wall as she stepped through the back door's exterior threshold. She immediately directed the flashlight to her feet. And combined with Jeff's beam to hers, a larger circumference came into view.

Back here, the sounds of crickets and a low vibrating hum filled the dark void. This had her quickly redirecting her beam of light back and forth as the unknown surroundings uncomfortably closed in on her. The sweeping movement revealed an enormous motorcycle several feet away from the doorway within the dome of illumination. Quickly following afterward, Allison laid the pile of bags near the bike.

With her abrupt stop, Jeff swung around her and started organizing the supplies into their proper storage compartments. When all the enclosed storage was filled, he secured the largest pouch to the back of the bike with an additional bungee cord and swung his frame over the seat.

A black helmet hung by its strap around the right side handlebar. Jeff smoothly scooped it up and effortlessly donned the head covering, displaying his familiarity with riding. Standing, holding both sides of the handlebars and balancing the bike between his legs, he looked back and gestured toward the one helmet remaining on the ground. "Go ahead, put yours on."

Allison reluctantly did as he instructed.

Jeff grinned at her and briefly waited as she struggled to fasten the helmet before slapping her hands away and pulling her closer.

He twisted slightly on the bike to use both hands and

diligently secured the helmet on her head. Once done, he pressed the button off to the side and activated the Bluetooth communication device in sync with his. Tapping once on the rounded, heavy-duty, plastic shell, he grinned. "Okay–now you get on," he said while bracing the bike and waiting.

When a few moments passed–and there was still no indication of her getting on the seat–Jeff twisted back around. "What's the hold-up?"

Allison continued to hesitate. "Come on," he laughed. "You survived the plane ride. This is a piece of cake. Besides, didn't you ride a bike with that teenager to the airport?" he reminded her.

"A moped," she pointed out while grabbing onto his shoulder. Almost stumbling while swinging one leg over the high seat, his hand steadied her as she straddled across the wide cushion and secured her position.

"This bike is much bigger." Her comment sounded out of breath

Jeff laughed. "Damn straight! Okay, hold on. Let's get out of here."

As he kick-started the bike and popped the clutch, Allison held on tight as they accelerated toward the final stretch of their journey. She looked out into the blur of the night's surroundings, surprised by the lively excitement swirling inside.

A delighted laugh escaped, expressing pleasure in the ride as her arms hugged the dependable figure before her.

****

James and Sean Patterson took the last turn off Newark Road onto Airport Way. Pulling up in a small, private school bus painted in the standard yellow color, they came to a stop by the only hangar structure around the New Garden Airport.

"Either they haven't arrived yet, or we missed them," Sean said while checking the surrounding area.

"I think we missed them. It is identical to the plane's image Becca sent us," James confirmed, his face pressed close to the side window, staring at the small plane nearly swallowed up by the hangar's dimly lit expansion. He jogged around the back and tested the back door. The handle turned without any restrictions and, with a slight pull, swung outward.

Sean came up to James' side. His older brother clicked on his pocket flashlight and directed the light inside. Everything remained still and quiet.

"I told you we should have come in fast," Sean complained. "That stupid bus couldn't get out of its own shadow."

James jogged inside and came to the small corporate jet. He reached up to the right side of the plane, lightly tapping the engine mount on the wing. It was still warm to the touch. He quickly gestured for his brother to follow him back out.

"If we did as you say, we would have been Swiss cheese in no time flat," James finally replied to his brother as he made for the exit. "Agent Jeffery Collins isn't one to mess with. Coming in with an unassuming, slow-moving target would allow us to get a word in edgewise before the bullets or our ride went flying."

James Patterson sighed while shining the beacon of light on the ground by the back door. "It was a long shot, anyway."

"Rebecca couldn't get the Flight plan to see where he planned on landing. He keeps everything close to his chest. Smart."

He squatted down and brushed his fingers across the tire marked left in the loose dirt. "We just know they wanted to rendezvous with Maxwell at Valley Forge. Josh and Brian had just cleared the other smaller airports in a sixty-minute circumference we thought to check out. This place is seventy minutes from Valley Forge."

James and Sean had passed several motorcycles when they turned off Route One onto Newark Road. "But they were all single riders," he muttered when noting only one tire trail heading out of the airport. "They went by West Baltimore Pike, out of here. Or we would have passed them. But from there, I have no clue where they went next."

He swiveled around to meet his brother's gaze. "Maybe you can do your magic and spot them off some traffic cameras and give us a starting point."

Sean nodded. "Damn, James. We can't catch a break. Whoever is orchestrating this group doesn't make mistakes. What if Becca-"

"Don't!" James commanded. His strong shields couldn't stop Sean's emotions from tearing into him. James' empathic ability shot icy shards of pain into his head.

Realizing the effect of his unguarded fear slipping out to his brother, Sean swung around. He moved his gaze across the empty fields until his emotions got held in check. After only a slight hesitation, he turned back and said, "Let's get out of here. I'll do some computer sleuthing on my laptop back on the bus."

"Copy," James said. He stood up and slipped each hand into a back pocket. He, too, needed a moment to get centered. The worry of getting his cover blown had more to do with leaving Rebecca unprotected in this nest of vipers than any danger to himself.

As his fingers pressed inside the right pocket of his jeans, they brushed up against a stiff stock paper. Pulling out the item, he discovered it was an unassuming business card with a Greek revival-styled building, a small picket fence, and gardens depicted in an inked drawing. The name on the card read John M. Pearce, Director of The Freedman's Village, a Division of the Virginia National Park Services. Below this title, it listed the address and phone number contact information.

He turned the paper over and saw two short sentences, and he jolted in place. Someone wrote a message in crisp, precise print penmanship.

Who owns more of the others' secrets?

Silence is golden.

James flipped the card stock over and studied the front face again.

Sean stopped at the entrance of the bus. Realizing his brother wasn't following him, he turned around and caught the frown on his brother's face. He quickly moved closer to James. "What's that?"

"I think we need to look further into this guy," James replied, handing his brother the business card.

"Do you think this means your cover's safe?" Sean asked, focusing on the front of the card after reading the short message.

James only nodded in reply as he headed for the bus. With the younger brother on James' heels, he quickly entered the old bus and took the front passenger seat behind the driver's seat.

Sean followed James in and took the available driver's seat. Swiveling around to face his brother, he handed back the card.

"Who is she?" James said while flicking that small business card against his thigh. If this action didn't reveal his excitement, one would only have to look up. There were fiery glints blazing bright in his icy blue eyes.

"Let's go. We need to find them," James ordered. He prayed they could intercept Mrs. Maxwell and the FBI agent. He hoped for a chance to talk and maybe even get them to stand down if possible.

Frank Marshall's orders remained clear. They must keep the Maxwells out of their enemy's hands at all costs.

He hadn't liked the option of keeping Maxwell's bride and best friend under lock and key. Even if he thought it beat the alternative.

No telling what influence the Sons of Liberty would have on Will if they held his wife or Agent Collins hostage. Maxwell's gift could be disastrous if it fell into the wrong hands.

Looking down at the card's front face, James realized they might have another play available. That Jennifer Daniels' trustworthiness may not lie in sync with their enemy it also didn't mean it lay with them. But it made James' situation hopeful.

James and Rebecca's cover could only do so much from within the enemy's camp. But now, they may have a better way cleared for them if the worst case happens.

Chapter Twenty-Four

Close to a half hour later, Jeff and Allison had traveled many miles on a dark and deserted road. Dips, hills, and curves of the two-lane roadway passed dense tree groupings with intermittent fields of freshly prepped dirt– getting ready for a new season of crops.

The haze from their motorcycle's headlights created a faint halo under the tree's budding canopy. With exposure to the elements, a chilled wind blew through them from the surrounding wooded area–smelling thick with growing greenery and nearby water sources.

"Where are we?" Allison shouted, leaning toward Jeff's left ear.

Jeff reached up and activated his comm device on his helmet before replying, "Back road going into Willowdale, heading to Spring City, past Phoenixville." Jeff chuckled when Allison squeezed him tighter when hearing him come through her helmet's speakers.

"Are you hungry?" he added a few moments later.

The rolling nausea of worrying about Will and the plane ride had eased when they landed. It helped when relaying the information to Will concerning the upcoming mission and his hesitance to proceed.

She realized she hadn't eaten anything that day. "Yeah, now that you mention it, I could use something to eat." God only knew what was in store for them later on tonight or tomorrow. It would be best to fuel up and get her body prepared for what would come up next.

Jeff coasted down Pikeland Avenue and steered left onto Main Street. Nearby loud music obscured the sound of the motorcycle's acceleration, helping them avoid curious glances.

The frequency of riders driving through this scenic area prompted Jeff to use this mode of transportation in the first place. The small town's rich music history attracted many music and art lovers to the four-block downtown area. So, the city was used to out-of-town traffic.

Their detour to pick up food only slightly delayed Jeff's estimated arrival. When he came out of a local steak shop ten minutes later, she couldn't believe it. Handing Allison two take-out bags, they got on their way without any problems.

Well, one issue did arise. But his passenger's difficulty

managing a smooth mount back on the bike while holding bags in her hands wasn't one he gave credence to as he reeved the bike's engine, popped the clutch, and merged with the flowing traffic.

When Allison's high-pitched squeal came through on his blue-tooth device, he just smirked, pressing down on the accelerator.

Turning off Bridge Street onto a side road, they came to an industrial site with a large old brick-faced warehouse and the surrounding outer buildings. The bike coasted to a stop alongside the entrance. Wide, stone pillars topped with an old-fashioned globe light sat on either side of a black, metal, closed gate.

A resonating white noise hum from a rush of water filled the air when the motorcycle's engine switched off. Jeff jumped off the bike but held onto the handlebar, allowing Allison to swing off behind him while holding their fast food take-out bags.

"I want to walk the bike up. Not draw attention." A set of keys rattled while being pulled from his front pocket. He slipped the key into an electronic device mounted on the left-side pillar and pushed down a sequential code on a punch-key device.

"Sure," Allison replied while looking around curiously. Nearby, a series of locks clicked and unfastened as the gate slid open. They both headed up the paved driveway on foot. "What's that water I hear?"

"The back of the property borders the Schuylkill River. Technically, we're in Royersford, Pennsylvania now and not Spring City."

"I thought you told Will we were meeting him at the townhouse." Allison followed Jeff inside the fenced perimeter, helping him close the gate.

Jeff walked the bike toward the large building. Allison, interested in any new information, kept close to him for his reply. "Townhouse is code for this place. If they're tracing his calls, he'll know to come here in a roundabout route."

"How roundabout? I thought he said he'd be here soon."

"He'll go by way of Conshohocken. He has a townhouse in his name, and it has an underground tunnel that dumps him out in an area where he can lose a tail if necessary."

"You're serious? An underground tunnel. Is it widely known? Won't they know to look out for him along its route?"

"Yes and no. The previous owner restored the tunnel years ago. The tunnel is a part of the Underground Railroad. It is common in the area. Although, as far as public knowledge goes, it is somewhat forgotten. He can slip into his home with some of his men, then leave them there to slip out unnoticed."

"Where's here?" Allison asked.

"This is an old, abandoned paper company's storage facility dating back to the 1950s. I bought it four years ago when Will and I were scouting the area a while back."

"It's yours? "The semi-lite area didn't hide her grimace after her words came out. It had been rude to ask him, and the highly expressive face tied Jeff into Allison's train of thought. Her curiosity about Jeff's finances, doubting the reality of something like this on his FBI salary, overtook her polite upbringing.

However, his easy grin instantly put her at ease.

"Being from old, family money has some advantages. However, like you, I prefer to make my own way. This place caught my eye. Will and I liked the small town of Spring City. It has lots of character in its architecture and its people. I'll take you to Chaplin's Music Cafe if we can. That band we heard playing while passing through is among many on any given night."

Catching the tail end of East Bridge Avenue before Jeff almost dumped her off the bike by speeding away, she had wished time and better circumstances allowed a daytime tour. From what her glance picked up, the early ninth-century architecture along Main Street would be a fun afternoon to browse and shop.

"What are you doing with this place?" She gestured to the enormous building with the hand holding the smaller of the two fast food bags.

"I don't like to see old historic buildings go to waste. I've been restoring it using a well-known architect in the area." He smiled innocently enough, but Allison caught the mischievous glint in his expression.

"Let me guess, Jake." Stopping briefly to put her hand on her hips, though losing the effectiveness when holding the bundles of greasy burgers. "Why the secret?"

Jeff shrugged before replying. "Maybe just being cautious. It works for us now. Anyway, several shell-corporation not directly related to me own the property's title, so they're untraceable. Even without the investigation, I like to have inconspicuous places to escape to. My family can be overwhelming sometimes, and I'm not ashamed to admit to disappearing a time or two to avoid them."

"God, I hear you on that one." A goofy facial expression accompanied an affectionate shoulder bump hitting him.

Toward the side of the warehouse, the grade sloped up significantly. The noticeable improvements to the property caught curious eyes as Allison climbed the new exterior stairs leading up to a loading dock and three overhead doors.

From the looks of things, Jeff wasn't planning on industrially reusing the building. The enclosed area had a simple but pleasing decorative wrought iron railing with three double swinging gates lining up with the location of the overhead doors. The ground was paved with flagstone in a simple, non-conforming pattern edged with a double-layered border of restored brick.

"This was a storage warehouse for the American Paper Company. It was one of three sites owned by the company from 1952 until 1985. This one, closer to the river, had easier access to the river's canal. The company used it for shipping in supplies and exporting their paper products. Until I bought it, this place was sold off and on as storage facilities for shipping companies. I had to get the ordinance changed from industrial to residential/business. A relatively easy process considering how many local workers I hired to complete the project."

Allison headed to the far end of the patio to view the property, dropping their bags of food on the nearest five outdoor dining sets evenly spaced across the courtyard.

The grounds appeared deserted but no longer abandoned. Evidence of recently finished renovations were scattered among new projects in different stages of completion. It was a smorgasbord of architectural magic.

Every sweeping glance around increased her interest in discovering more about the property.

Jeff activated the security pad near a single exterior door.

"Gosh, I'm impressed." Allison stepped onto her toes and leaned slightly over the guardrail to take it all in. A small two-story outbuilding with a fenced-in yard caught her notice. The rod iron scroll design of the fence matched the design she was currently leaning on.

An excited murmur escaped. Her delight became quickly expressed when she spied a massive organic-shaped in-ground pool surrounded by lush plantings standing out among rolling hills with neatly cut lawns.

The grounds held discreet but efficient exterior lighting on historically reproduced pole lights; similar but smaller than the two pillar's lights by the front gage. These lights consistently edged several well-groomed paths through picturesque walking trails and direct service routes. Numerous in-ground uplights perfectly accentuated the serpentine river, and the neatly sculptured landscape, plus the natural terrain of the property's borders, gave beautiful backdrops.

A smooth, mechanical humming sound had her pivoting away from the awe-inspiring views.

Catching Jeff bending down to duck the center overhead door as it rose, she gleefully rubbed her hands briskly together before snatching up the food and hurrying inside.

Jeff brought the bike up a small side ramp, closed the overhead doors, and reset the security alarm.

Stepping inside, Allison couldn't control her shocking gasp at the overall effect of the beautifully executed restoration. It enhanced the historical features while intermixing an eclectic design for the new construction and furnishings.

A full circle spin encompassed it all, and the most amazing surprise happened. Allison's past input and ideas reflected back in the interior design work throughout.

"I can't believe it!" she yelled excitedly, slapping Jeff on the arm numerous times and bouncing up and down on her toes.

Chapter Twenty-Five

Rebecca's cell phone vibrated while Sara was getting a bath before dinner. The clear suspicion of that little girl being part fish due to her affinity for water still rang true. Spending most of the day in the pool with her mom and later with her Aunt Peg, Uncle Bob, Mee-maw Bettie, Bob's mother, and Rebecca wasn't enough. She had to linger in the bath, as well, with no hint of slowing down.

Rebecca wiped the bubbles from her hands and pulled out her phone to see the caller ID. She angled her body toward Peggy, Allison's very energetic sister. "I need to take this call."

"No problem, I'll finish here and meet you downstairs for dinner." Peg giggled at her niece. Sara had scooped up a bunch of the bubbles, smearing them all over her face while puffing out her cheeks full of air, making pursed, fish lips.

"Okay... Thanks." Rebecca got up from the floor next to the tub. Her capris were now soaked around to the knees. "I'm definitely wearing my wetsuit next time." Rebecca chuckled while exiting the room. She tucked into her bedroom directly across the hallway and answered the call.

"Special Agent Patterson." Her voice cautiously lowered to a whisper.

"Good evening, Agent Patterson. Edward Sharpe speaking. I have orders which are to be carried out immediately."

"What do you want?" The grip on her phone tightened. She had known this call would come; she had hoped to avoid it.

"We need Sara and Allison delivered in the next few hours."

Not having any other option, she stalled. "I don't know if I can accomplish that request. Sara is here with me, but I'm unsure of Allison's whereabouts."

"Why not?"

"I reported earlier to my handler that Agent Collins and Allison left to meet with Will," she told him.

"Do you have a way to contact her?" His manner was veiled in annoyance.

She hesitated before answering, "Yes."

"Good. Call Mrs. Maxwell and get her to meet you at this location.

"I'll contact you within the hour… No, wait, I'll have the address sent through a text message with a phone number to contact when you have the child secured. Wait in Washington, DC, for further instructions. Call your contact for pick up. You know what will happen if you fail." Sharpe enjoyed making the threat.

"Yes, I'm well aware of the consequences." She sighed heavily as the call ended. She turned off her phone as she plopped down on her bed. Tugging open the drawer of the nearby table, she reached inside, mindlessly searching the underside of the tabletop with her fingers. With touch-tactile movements, she located the duct tape that secured her additional cell phone and carefully ripped it away.

Pulling it out and turning it on, she had to wait for the hardware to boot. It seemed like forever before she could push the programmed speed dial number. The line was picked up on the first ring.

"They made contact," she confided softly. "What are your orders?"

The soaked clothing pulled at her skin. Moving to her dresser, she opened the bottom drawer and pulled out a dry pair of pants. With the phone tucked between her ear and shoulder, she began undressing.

It didn't take long for the special ops handler to demand all the pertinent information.

"Yes. As we suspected, Sharpe made adjustments due to the change of plans at Valley Forge. I couldn't get Agent Collins to go with Maxwell initially." Rebecca kicked off the sneakers and resumed changing her pants. "I'm to notify my Copperhead contact for transportation out of here."

A short pause occurred before she continued, "One hour. Arrangements are needed for the family." Another pause before adding, "Copy. I'll notify my backup. Agent Patterson out."

She ended the call and immediately texted the safe house information for her ride.

Right after that conversation, she called out to her brothers through their private telepathic communication link. And like before, a reply didn't take long.

Sis, what's up?

Her brother Josh's nonchalant greeting was just a front to a well-oiled, no-nonsense, and intensely controlled demeanor that she would be desperately counting on for the next few days.

It's a go. I'm to bring Sara to them. My ride will be here in one hour. Were you successful in finding Allison and Agent Collins?

No. They left before James and Sean got there. Sean couldn't locate them on any traffic cams in the surrounding area. They must've taken back roads. Josh Patterson replied.

The extended family is here. I compromised the safe house by contacting my Sons of Liberty contact for a pickup. I can't count on Pete and the remaining agents right now to keep the house secured. Jeff–I mean, Agent Collins trusts them, but I'm not taking any chances. You need to get here. Secure the team and family. She relayed to her brother.

Josh relayed back: *You're a go for backup. They were on standby as we planned. They'll get there well before twenty-one-fifteen. We'll make sure no surprises occur. We will detain the team they leave behind when they send your transportation. Sean arranged a new location for the family. We were waiting for your signal.*

Good to know. Rebecca sighed and added. *Since you guys couldn't find Jeff and Allison, they'll be accessible to Sharpe's maneuverings.*

Unfortunately, yes. Josh's tone sounded heavy in her mind.

Rebecca sighed. It had been a long shot anyway, but she had hoped for the best. She didn't want Allison mixed up with these thugs. But now it didn't look like anyone could prevent it. *Well, we tried. I'll be ready to do my part.*

Sis? Josh added. His tone turned soft-spoken.

Yeah?

Be careful. Sean will shadow you. Don't take any chances. Josh's thoughts shot out with such force behind them that they vibrated in his sister's mind.

Count on it. Out.

They severed their connection.

Rebecca looked at her watch to confirm the time before

moving into action.

With calm but hurried movements, she got her packed duffle bag out of the closet and secured the secondary phone inside. She zipped and buttoned her pants, slipped back into her sneakers, and headed out the door.

In the next several hours, she had a lot to accomplish.

The first thing was getting a large cup of coffee. Because sleep just became the least of her priorities.

****

Allison couldn't stop touching everything while Jeff stood nearby, grinning from ear to ear. "Did you know I worked on this?" She shifted and waited for Jeff's response, already suspecting the outcome.

"Yep." He smirked. "Will bankrolled the renovation. He insisted on your feedback. I couldn't wait to see your face when you got here. And why I strongly disagreed with you earlier. What you provide for your clients is a gift. And I, for one, am very grateful for your talents."

"Jake told me it was for a competition we were entering. The likelihood of the proposed warehouse restoration for elite executive apartments with a social lounge, dining room, and a bar built on the premise, passing the current zoning laws, was minuscule," Allison explained, walking around and trailing her fingers across the many surfaces. "That rat fink! I never doubted him when he said it fell through."

The gleaming polished original plank flooring sparkled beneath the industrial decorative pendant fixtures, suspended from the multiple ceiling soffits and the expanded clerestory atrium The building could easily fit the length of one football field front to back and from side to side and then some.

"He really did it!" Allison exclaimed, taking in all the surrounding improvements.

One of the remaining exterior walls showcased the original facade, boasting a three-tiered arrangement of arched top windows. A full clerestory bank adorned just below the exposed-beamed peaked roof. On the opposite end, a pre-existing mezzanine level seamlessly bridged the new construction with the existing restoration.

"You kept the original warehouse mezzanine level, attaching the new construction on both sides. God, I'm so glad." Squealing delightfully, Allison jumped up and down while grabbing Jeff's arm tightly. "This is gorgeous! I want to live here."

Jeff laughed. "You do."

Allison jolted before pivoting around to question his sanity.

"Will partnered with me on the project, plus he has one of the penthouse units, Mrs. Maxwell," Jeff informed her with a huge grin dominating his expression.

He pointed to the original mezzanine structure. On the right stood a contemporary glass-enclosed elevator at the end of the atrium space near the back wall with open-design grand staircases mirrored on both sides. "I set it up as condominium, rental units, and high-end amenity services. I don't believe in hiding places that don't make a profit."

"Okay... come on, I can't wait to see your place." She shot off a series of questions in a rushed manner while pulling him along. "Is it two levels like Jake designed? Did he go with the Moroccan stone countertops for the Main Suite's Bathroom? And did he use the recycled, plastic-composite product for all the private balconies?" Allison grinned from ear to ear, still finding it hard to believe that this place actually existed.

Jeff's slow nod, glazed-over eyes, and slacked jaw had her chuckling.

They entered his place using the new glass-enclosed elevator with its own security code, followed by additional security measures by his apartment entryway. "Will designed the security systems throughout the property. It's his design–separate from Guardians Inc.," Jeff explained as he keyed in a code to release the front door.

Allison, too impatient, skipped around him to see inside. This was a nice reprieve from all the intense situations happening, and she wanted to enjoy it.

She dropped the food down onto the kitchen counter,

hopefully for the very last time, and spun in a slow circle. It became hard to believe that what she thought was picked out for fictitious furniture and finish sample boards stood all around them in all its true glory.

A sinfully soft, hand-rubbed, leather sectional sofa and trendy faux-fur beanbag chairs faced the widescreen TV, which hung mounted onto the brick-faced double-facing fireplace. The room successfully incorporated the quirky, sophisticated style reflected in the lobby's common areas with some personal effects that Jeff must have added. Allison remembered what fun it had been to design an energetic and non-traditional space.

"I guess I did some good while hiding myself away," she unknowingly spoke those thoughts out loud. Hurrying from the open living space to the intimate corner near the tall casement windows, she oohed and aahed, touching everything in sight.

"Yeah. You totally did," Jeff replied, finding himself a little dizzy watching her sprint from one point to the next.

She finally plopped down onto an incredibly soft cashmere-covered cushion adhered to a free-formed, pressed bamboo Scandinavian recliner.

Resting her hands on either side of her reposed position, she gently smoothed them along the soft fabric. "Don't you just love this chair? Not only is it sooo comfortable... it's a piece of art, too!"

"Umm, I guess." Jeff, being a guy, didn't get it.

"Okay, designer Allison, I need the field agent Allison, to return and get to work."

Her eyes popped open, spotting Jeff rummaging through the food while wearing his customary smug expression.

"Lucky for you, I can do both," she said while smirking right back at him. "What do you need?"

Chapter Twenty-Six

After hurried footsteps and a quick knock, the door swung open. Michael Arenald stood just inside the room to greet the new arrival.

Jennifer Daniels caught her breath and stopped short of hitting his imposing presence waiting within. A quick grin appeared on her face before Michael enveloped her in a warm hug.

But the large, cumbersome bag, a constant companion, slipped from her shoulder and interrupted their embrace.

"What kept you, Little Miss?" He stepped back and swung his hand around to gesture toward the small table. One to-go cup with a corrugated cardboard sleeve to protect from the coffee's heated liquid inside sat beside a brown paper bag.

"I had to lose a tail," she replied as her attention was drawn to Michael's gift. Recognizing the white and blue muffin-shaped logo on the cup and the bag, Jennifer fondly smiled at the small treat while heading to the table. A slight jolt interrupted her forward motion when she spotted the other occupant leaning against the sidewall.

Michael, very much attuned to this particular lady's body language, quickly made introductions. "Ms. Daniels meet Miles Jennings. He had a lot to do with getting the information from our warehouse intruders and the Guardians Inc.'s guards. I brought him along due to his inside knowledge of Sharpe's habits."

Stiffly pushing off the wall, he pulled off the earpods, placed them around his neck, and switched off his music. He was still reeling over Black arranging a replacement MP3 player ready for him when he stepped off the ferry. What was even more impressive were the songs already downloaded onto the device. Someone prepared all his favorite sets ready to play.

Miles' right hand reached outward as he invited, "Call me MJ."

Jennifer took his hand and shook briskly before dropping down into the available seat. She dug into her canvas bag, pulling out a notebook and pen. A red ribbon tucked more than halfway through the journal's depths marked the next available page.

A quick flick of her fingers had the pages fanning open and a clean sheet ready to go. Her gaze darted to the informant, and the pen was poised ready to take notes. After a short pause when no one spoke, Jennifer's eyebrows lifted, and her lips pursed.

MJ gingerly took his seat before beginning a lengthy dialogue about the men's identities, where they came from, and whose company they kept since entering Sharpe's employment.

Very detailed notes in small but neat penmanship–resembling a strange form of shorthand–spanned several sheets of paper before MJ got to the interesting part.

"Course, as suspected, Sharpe ordered his blokes to keep tabs on Black's movements." MJ's attention kept centered on Jennifer. She nodded her head up and down as he explained how little information the tails had managed to gather. Her pen lifted, and she gestured with her hand in a rolling wave, knowing something important still needed to be said.

MJ cleared his throat before mentioning, "If an assassination attempt became possible, making no pig's ears back to Sharpe, they were to seize the opportunity. A mess of P's would go to any man who did the job. Umm, five mils. Yeah, lots of dosh, mate. Not much more-"

"Which explains the attack on Mr. Black." Jennifer's careful persona dropped for an instant when coming to a realization. "You're the agent that saved him, aren't you?" Her gaze flickered to MJ, spotting the careful stance of his posture. She cleared her throat. Took a sip from her coffee and directed her gaze to the wall behind him. "Thank you." A flash of warmth filled her eyes before the all-business persona fell right back firmly in place.

Miles dropped his gaze to the tabletop. "I got lucky, is all. No thanks, required." He darted his gaze at numerous items in the room. "Anyway..." He coughed and eased carefully backward, leaning against his chair's back.

"Tell her about what the mercenary overheard when Sharpe took a call from Nancy Johnson in his company and what Maxwell's guards confirmed," Michael prompted.

Nodding, MJ quickly sat forward and added, "Someone with Maxwell's last name wanted his P's before he made the call to Will. Something about a well-timed iron in the fire. The guards did corroborate that this particular insider might contact them for possible orders, but they never received any direct commands. They didn't know his name." Miles' chuckle escaped, and he gave Ms. Daniels a smirk. "But Sharpe said this contact would have a code name, Mr. Pink, if he did get in touch with them."

Jennifer tilted her head to the side before twisting in her seat to meet Michael's gaze. "There are no Maxwell family members in the Sons of Liberty or Copperheads that I know of. Whoever this is seems to be working directly for Sharpe."

Black's trusted companion slowly nodded, realizing the seriousness of this new development. "I started looking at phone records on everyone surrounding William Maxwell. I'm told it will take some time to find any connection back to Sharpe, and that it may be a long shot. He may have used a burner phone we don't know about." Michael brought his phone out from his front pocket and continued coordinating with the delegated resources made available to them.

Jennifer turned back and addressed MJ, "Those mercenaries' phones?"

After knocking on the table surface a few times with his knuckles, MJ braced himself for the jolt when standing. The healing ability still left him with muscles that protested any movement. But it wasn't even in the same ballpark as to what his body suffered after he came back from when Sharpe threw him in the New River.

He shook off that morbid note and gave Jennifer a reply. "We have several phones that got pinched from the warehouse. I'll take a punt and give them another pass. Once Michael gets the list of Sharpe's and Maxwell's numbers, we'll gander another look. Maybe we'll get jammy and find something."

"Good. I'm on my way to The Freedom Village. I'll be there until Sunday night. Contact Michael if you need to get a hold of me. Let's hope we get a lead." Jennifer carefully placed the ribbon between the next clean page of her notebook.

She was ever so thankful that Black approved her idea of contacting James Patterson and giving him that hint to that particular Sons of Liberty's hideout. By this time, she hoped he had received her message. Even knowing how precarious this move could prove–possibly biting her in the butt down the road–she still trusted her gut. By giving the Patterson Brothers an edge, she still believed it beat the alternative.

If William Maxwell and his new family became hostages, that facility would most likely house them. Jennifer needed a way to rescue them, along with Andrew McKnight, without breaking her cover.

She quickly dropped the leather journal in her canvas tote and swept it onto her shoulder. Her gaze fell to the take-out bag.

Her stomach revolted with the thought of food, but she knew Michael went out of his way to pick up a blueberry scone from her favorite coffee shop. She wouldn't hurt his feelings for any reason in the world. "Michael, I will keep this delightful treat for when I get to the museum."

Michael, having completed several quick phone calls, met her leveled, calm expression and nodded back. "Don't skip another meal, Little Miss."

Jennifer Daniels gave a small smile. She had no desire to lie. But lifting the coffee cup, she said, "I'm going to swig down this hazelnut latte as soon as I get on the bus."

Her grin faded as the seriousness of the situation returned. "If someone around William Maxwell is dirty, then they can get to him easier than we thought. We need to know when they plan on playing that card. And we need to know soon."

****

A high-resonated beep alerted Allison and Jeff to the arriving company. Jeff entered a room off the kitchen and switched on the lights. The security monitors recessed in a large custom millwork desk displayed several interior and exterior shots around the property.

Allison leaned on the counter's surface beside Jeff, watching the multiple views.

"He's here." Jeff tapped on the screen that showed someone shutting the gate and re-engaging the lock.

"How do you know it's him?" Allison asked.

Jeff tapped his forehead and answered, "He just said, 'open the damn door'."

"I didn't know he rode a motorcycle." Her weight shifted from one leg to the next. She bit down on one nail while watching the rider disappear off one screen, only to reappear on another. Not long afterward, Will punched in a security code at the back entrance that allowed access to the interior foyer leading to their private elevator.

Waiting for Will became so unbearable she went back to the kitchen.

The bag of burgers were unloaded, unwrapped from their foiled-back paper, and separated from the breading. Rummaging through the upper cabinets, she came across a microwavable plate and stacked the burgers before placing them in the microwave to reheat.

Will spotted Allison as soon as he walked in, but his obstinate wife purposely didn't turn around. A cooking timer went off, and he watched as a cooking tray was retrieved sitting nearby. Only after carefully transferring a steaming stack of meat patties out from the microwave onto that other metal holder did she turn toward him and place the food down on the counter between them.

Allison caught his gaze, then switched her attention back to the food. The burgers were reassembled with slow, careful movements.

Jeff entered the kitchen and headed for the stainless-steel Sub-Zero refrigerator out of Will's peripheral vision. No one spoke as the side door opened, and Jeff grabbed various drinks. The refrigerator's door slammed with a swooshing sound as Jeff's hip bumped it shut, and he moved across the spacious layout to place the beverages on the counter next to their food. Upon smelling the take-out, his stomach growled loudly.

Three burgers and his preferred soft drink were snatched up while saying, "I'm taking a shower. You two goofy feet take the drop, and no grubbing. When I get back, we'll carve out a clean wave." Leaning over to kiss Allison's cheek, he whispered. "Men are all he-man fools. Go easy on him, but if that doesn't work, Betty... you always have me."

A weak chuckle escaped Allison's lips, having some clue on what he said–but barely.

Jeff's footsteps eased down the hallway, and soon after, a door clicked softly closed. She stood alone with Will. "Are you hungry?" she quietly asked.

"No."

*Okay, here we go. S*he thought. Reassembling more burgers, she had something to do while waiting for the explosion. *One... two... three-*

"What the hell were you thinking, Ally?" Pacing back and forth, he spewed out his frustration. "I wanted you to stay put at the safe house. I've been out of my mind with worry, wondering where you got to." He halted his pacing to rest his fists on his hips, glaring. "And Sara. What about Sara? When was the last time you spoke with her?"

Allison walked away from him to wash her hands at the kitchen sink. She spun back around with a tea towel fisted in her hands. Releasing the mangled fabric, she began folding the mussed cloth into small squares, attempting to press out the wrinkles.

She took a deep breath and responded, "No. Will, I haven't spoken to Sara since we left around 6:00 this evening. My sister and her family arrived just after we left. Because, you know. When you thought your capture was possible, you sent for them, thinking we would have someone to lean on." She allowed a short pause for Will to respond but none came. "So… I'm sure having Peggy and her family there pleasantly occupies our daughter."

Leaning against the counter, hugging her waist, she continued in a calm voice that hid the raging volcano bubbling up to the surface. "Of course, Sara is probably already in bed now. Rebecca or Peg will help her FaceTime me tomorrow when she wakes up."

A loud rumbling originated from her stomach. Figuring it was hard for someone to take her seriously while sounding like an animated Muppet character, she grabbed a burger and took a large bite. The chewing on the reheated patty gave her jaw a workout, but it tasted delicious. Probably due to her being half-starved. "I'm sorry you were worried, but you left me no choice.

"You left," Allison huffed. "You broke your promise, Will… and lied to me numerous times. I know what you do is dangerous, and every time you do your job, there is a chance that you could get hurt. However, taking unnecessary risks should be open to discussion. Our decision." She pressed her empty hand against her chest before adding, "Was decided when a threat to your plan-" The hand holding her burger waved toward Will in an exasperated manner. "An idiotic plan, if you ask me, became exposed."

Her calm and direct statements tore through all his blustering anger, which had been a cover for his fear. It cut him to the core, thinking of her in danger. Will took a deep breath and exhaled slowly. He averted his gaze from her. The hurt he caused was clearly reflected in her expression. This brought him heartache.

The budding trust he had managed to build between them was now strained.

It required fixing.

"I'm sorry, Ally. I did lie to you," Will said as he flopped down on the hard, clear acrylic barstool. Arms bent, elbows leaning on the counter, he rested his chin on an open palm. The pads of his fingers drummed against a cheekbone. "How mad at me are you?"

"On a scale from one to ten, I started at twelve earlier today and have simmered down to a... six. Now that I have something in my stomach, and you're safe with us." She took another bite of her burger while slightly mimicking his pose.

"I'm also confused about why you didn't tell me about working for my uncle." Her voice dropped in volume. They stood nose to nose across the counter.

Will looked away, stiffly explaining, "I tried to tell you several times, but we constantly got interrupted." He pulled his gold coin from his front pocket. Rubbing the embossed face centered his emotions.

He brought his gaze back to hers. His voice lowered a little more, a calming tone coating every word. "Guardians, Inc. got hired by your uncle when I transferred to Washington, DC. I had assigned two teams to shadow you and your sister, giving me updates. Those reports were sent to me, and I decided what information got forwarded to your uncle.

"I should have told you, Ally," Will confessed while playing with the gold coin. "It was stupid of me not to say something right off the bat. My only excuse is that you've managed to throw me through a loop from that initial meeting with Debbie and Jake, and I haven't been on my game since. And this latest snafu of mine just wanted to keep you safe, too." He released a pent-up breath as his shoulders slumped in defeat.

Studying his appearance, she saw the regret. Knowing his need to stay in control, on top of keeping the people he cared about safe, would heavily influence him and often blur the lines with personal boundaries. Loving him would mean accepting all the facets of his personality and preparing to find a new path forward that they both agreed on.

Shrugging her shoulders, she took a deep breath and released it. "Okay. But I want things done differently from now on. No secrets," she sternly demanded.

Grinning at her, he reached across the space between them and peeled off the fake facial hair she still had on her.

She giggled. "Oops," she said while pulling off the bandana and shaking her hair out.

"If it's any consolation, I thought the risk was worth having this situation over and behind us. I don't want to stay in this limbo. I want my life back with you and Sara." He cupped her cheek with his free hand in a soft caress.

"I know that, Will, but we should have discussed it."

"You would have said no," Will sheepishly said while stepping back. His hand dropped down to rest on the countertop.

A surprised laugh escaped before she said, "Damn right! I would have, just like Jeff. You aren't thinking straight to have agreed to something like this."

Tears pooled until they finally spilled over unheedingly down her cheeks. She swiped them away. "Will, it is a real trap. Director Campbell is not who you think. Jeff can tell you more, but the risk of a real capture was very high if we hadn't interfered. I was so scared. You're not indestructible. And with the Curse..."

"Baby, there is no such thing as a curse-" Will spotted her gearing up to argue and quickly switched tactics. "But you're right about being more careful. I'm sorry." Coming around the other side of the counter, he got close to her and held her in a warm embrace. Her shoulders began heaving with the release of suppressed emotions.

Squeezing him tighter, she tried to control her spiraling reaction, but it became impossible to contain once set free. "I don't knoo–waa–what's wronn–g..." A hiccup escaped. "I–ahh, ca- caa–nnt –stooop." Her shoulders continued shaking with her heavy sobs.

Even as he stood before her unharmed, she felt an overwhelming panic take hold.

Chapter Twenty-Seven

Will gently pulled back from Allison, spying a bundle of napkin beside the take-out bag. He wiped at her streaming tears. "Have some more of your burger, Ally. Your sugar is probably low from not eating all day."

Allison grabbed her unfinished burger. She concentrated on taking small bites and swallowing them with a flavored seltzer drink that Will had opened for her.

However, each time her crying settled down to a slight hiccup, the tears would return, and the sobs would start all over again. "I don't knno–oow what's wrong with me," she mumbled while wiping away more tears. The napkin pieces stuck to her face, where the disguised facial hair adhesive hadn't worn off yet. She started to laugh, but it morphed back into sobs.

Walking into the kitchen, Jeff toweled off his hair and readily took in the scene. He approached Allison, holding the towel's corner up to her nose, and told her to blow. "It's totally normal, Ally," Jeff explained as he patted her shoulder affectionately.

"You've been caught inside and carving the wave all day. You're not dinged. Everything is just catching up with you." Walking to the sink, he wet the other corner of his towel, added some soap, and returned to wash her face. "You'll need an alcohol swab to get the residue off your chin." He smiled while gently scrubbing away some of the adhesive. "I like you so much better as a lady."

Will tightened his embrace. "So do I," he whispered in her ear. "Why don't you take a shower while Jeff fills me in on what I missed?"

Jeff retrieved the leather satchel he had set down on the sofa. "Here are your clothes. Take that shower. We'll wait for you to come back to finalize the plan. The second door on the left is a guest bedroom with its own bath. Take your things and settle in there."

"Don't decide anything without me." She pivoted, facing Will, holding and squeezing the duffel bag before her like a child would her favorite stuffed animal when needing comfort.

"I promise," Will stated solemnly. With his hand over his heart, he looked like he was about to recite the pledge of allegiance. "We'll come up with one together."

"All right then." Allison hugged the satchel to her chest and made her feet take one step after another down the hall. Her movements were sluggish, like walking through soupy air.

"Ally, the alcohol pads are in the medicine cabinet," Jeff called out to her.

"Kay…" She sniffled while continuing down the hall.

Angling toward his good friend, Jeff held both ends of the towel as it hung around his neck. "That's one amazing woman you have there. If she didn't love you so damn much, I'd charge that wave and take her from you."

"I know." Then, with a short grunt, he added, "As a matter of fact, I don't think so. I have a feeling a certain red-headed agent holds your true interest."

Jeff discovered another burger while poking through the take-out bag, choosing to ignore Will's asinine insight. Gesturing toward the burger, he asked. "You want?" With Will's hand gesturing refusal, Jeff unwrapped and then destroyed the burger under three mouthfuls.

Scarfing down the last bite, he studied his friend. "Will… you are one lucky bastard. This was a chunder move."

Will took a page from Jeff's approach on the available seating and jumped onto the nearby countertop. He directed his full attention onto Jeff and waited.

His partner looked at the place on the countertop–where Will currently resided–and then spied Will's glaring look. A quick cocky grin flashed across Jeff's face.

Crossing his arms together, Will rested them on his chest and waited out his friend. It didn't take long before Jeff's expression turned serious.

"I'm positive Campbell is a mole. I started snooping around after you made your stupid ass decision. He moved up in the ranks pretty damn fast. Looking into his background, which took some doing–by the way, I found discrepancies similarly noted in other disappearances surrounding this group. His younger sister went missing a year ago. The same M.O. afterward. Campbell said they spoke to her, and she was taking time to travel. All trials led to that declaration, and they dropped the missing person's case. As soon as that came across my desk, I made the call to join you. I was denied by my superior, saying it came down from Campbell. Thanks to the asinine stipulation you set in place. So, yeah. I assembled my team, which took a few hours."

"Then, Allison, being Allison," Will surmised.

Jeff grinned and added, "Caught onto the situation, and started her own campaign. Damn, Will, she stayed up in the cockpit the whole time, trying to understand everything about flying a plane during the flight." His head tilted upward toward the ceiling.

"With everything that's happened in the last few days, she's gonna close out. When she comes back, let's go 'Inside The Greenroom', and let her kick out."

Will's eyes blinked a few times while translating Jeff's words before shaking his head in agreement. Allison was operating on very little sleep because of him. But the trick would be not suggesting anything; that would only end in a refusal. His gut gave out vibes that things were coming to a head.

"I intercepted some new transmissions through one of my cyber-sweeps, but nothing concrete. These Croatian terrorist groups are not disclosing any specific details regarding their back and forth communications with each other. There is chatter about Andrew McKnight. More importantly, Sean sent me a text that they may have a strong lead. He and his brother want to check it out first before disclosing more. He also believes that James' cover is safe." He went through the little bit of specifics that came through his searches. But it wasn't enough to fill in any of those missing gaps. We need to get our hands on someone with more information," Will said.

"There's a heavy push to flush out the leaks and the moles in our backyard," Jeff added. "The multiple divisions are concentrating on nailing any Sons of Liberty's spies. It's a smart move. We are just chasing our tails if we leave it alone."

"Then we should reconsider scrapping the Valley Forge snare. It could still work, but let's shift the concentration on catching the moles in our teams. If we get any Sons of Liberty's associates in the net, all the better."

They were batting around some ideas when they heard the door down the hall open and then close.

"Hey! You guys. You promised no brainstorming until I got back." Allison ran down the hall in her leggings and a long-sleeved T-shirt. Her hair was still wet and combed away from her face. She looked clean and flushed pink from a hot shower.

"No worries, honey," Will reassured her while figuring out a way to get her to consider resting. "We were just throwing things around until you got back. I'm operating on only three hours of sleep–so if we manage it, I could use a few hours to rest."

"Oh, okay…" Allison wrapped her arms around Will and tucked her face into his chest.

Jeff's gaze locked with Will's, and he winked while Allison wasn't looking. *Bitchin' clever- dude.* Jeff's comment went through their internal telepathic connection.

Will's internal communication of, *I'm no Grom!* Hit with a heavy push into Jeff's mind.

Unaware of their silent banter, Allison interrupted. "What did you guys toss around?"

Jeff plopped down on the far left side of the sectional and explained. "Will still wants to try the Valley Forge bait but with one major revision. Instead of relying on Director Campbell's team, we'll use our own team of agents and private security personnel to catch them in the act."

"Well, as long as you have plenty of coverage for Will," Allison said, watching Will move into the sitting area on the opposite side of the sectional.

Pleasantly pleased to see him ease aside the decorative pillows, Allison smiled, charmed by her husband. In the past week, she had mentioned enough times about decorative pillows being visual accents only and not to squash them when sitting.

Making sure her shields stayed locked in place she allowed her inner thoughts to escape. *How lucky would I be if my husband was as easily trainable on other things as well? Like just adjusting that tendency toward being a tad bit overprotective.* Allison grinned.

"No- we should have it covered." Will looked up and saw Allison hovering just outside the seating area. Moving the pillows even farther away, he patted the seat beside him. "If Jeff sets up a perimeter of our own people, I'll follow the director's plan.

"Just to be safe, we'll install a transmitter with a specialized signal that Jeff can pick up. You can listen in at all times and be able to track my location if something goes wrong."

Allison studied them both. Sprawled across the sectional, each dominated the sofa's opposite sides. She maneuvered around Will's legs and squeezed by to sit near him. "Hopefully, you have an army of men you trust."

Will shrugged. "I can't be 100% positive on all fronts, Ally. What happened back in Orlando was certainly a wake-up." He was referring back to when Jeff, Will, and a team of agents chased Allison to Florida. During that retrieval, they discovered two of Guardian's Inc.'s men had been working for the Copperheads.

But since then, Will and Jeff double-checked the Guardians, Inc.'s agents with high-level clearances. So far, no standing red flags, but that only got them so far. There was always a chance they missed someone.

Sighing while her shoulders slumped inward, she fell back to the back cushion in a dramatic flair. Will chuckled briefly before lifting her onto his lap and kissing her forehead.

Both Jeff and Will took the time to explain how the trap would work in great detail. After numerous tweaks–and incorporating some of Allison's excellent points–the plan was finalized within a half hour or so later.

Although, if Allison had her way, they would have doubled the team around Will. After repeating that request numerous times, Will calmly responded, "Ally, I can't have an army hanging around me. They'd suspect a trap. Twelve people, covering a forty-foot radius, should do it." Will took Allison's hand and squeezed gently.

She frowned and gave another loud sigh. Partly out of frustration but mainly because the day's activities were finally catching up with her.

Seeing the fatigue set in on his wife, Will coaxed, "You're tired. Why don't you lay down with me?"

"Because. As soon as I fall asleep, you're going to leave," she fired back.

Will chuckled, and that sexy timbre resonated through her entire upper body. "Come on, smarty pants. I'll stay a couple of hours with you, then head back to my place." He did it for himself as much as for her. Will needed to feel Allison in his arms.

"Fine..." Adjusting around to see if Jeff would mind, she chuckled, finding him asleep. Will pushed her up off his lap, and she reached for the throw draped along the back cushions near her husband's best friend. She carefully placed it across Jeff's upper body.

Waiting nearby, Will outstretched his hand toward his wife. He tugged her closer when her hand settled in his. Walking hand in hand, they headed for their room.

The condo fell into a more profound quiet. Just the background noises from a plethora of sources kept the rooms alive. A hum from the air-conditioned system running through the vents throughout, the mechanical tick-tock from the clock hanging on the kitchen wall, and a slight snore emanating from the living room eased the environment from dangerous plots to everyday normal.

She counted on them all having a small respite from this challenging case but seriously doubted that the stars would align to make it happen. After all, they hadn't so far, and the situation looked to be coming to a head at any moment.

Chapter Twenty-Eight

Acell phone rang on a coffee table nearby. A hand struggled to locate it while still half asleep. Answering the call, he groggily spoke into the device. "Agent Collins speaking."

"Hey, it's Agent Patterson. I didn't wake you, did I?" Her sarcastic and unapologetic tone caused the exact warranted response.

"What do you want, Miss Thorn-in-my-side?" he responded while easing up, more awake now.

"I didn't hear back from Allison; I'm just checking in."

His fingers skimmed the soft textile that currently covered him. Warmth gathered in his heart for his best friend's mate. Jeff never imagined he would crave something like what he saw in Will and Allison for himself.

But he also couldn't get it out of his head that a certain Special Agent was perfect for him. *That's if we ever get our timing right.*

"We are good. Bossman will probably return to his location no later than zero-one-hundred (1:00 a.m.). He's trying to get Allison to take a break."

"I'll call back later. What time would work?" Her tone sounded a little distracted.

"Give her some time, say around zero hundred (midnight). She'll be up by then. We need to pound out a couple last-minute details for tomorrow."

"Copy. Patterson out. Jeff?" she added softly.

"Yeah?"

A long pause drew out for several moments before a soft sigh proceeded her comment, "Um ah. I was a smart ass earlier. You get some rest and take care."

"Copy. Thanks. Rebecca don't let the little imp run you ragged. Although, with all your nieces and nephews, you certainly are familiar with the madness. See you later."

"Later," she replied. Sighing again, she disconnected the call. Rebecca hated lying to him. She feared he would never understand and forgive her for what she had to do.

She shifted to her brother, Josh, and caught him, giving her a funny look. She shook her head in response. "You caught it all?"

He slowly nodded. His gaze held firmly to hers. "Is there

anything that I should know about? Anything regarding this Agent Collins that could compromise the mission?"

Rebecca's jaw clenched tight, and her head tilted to the side. An all too familiar stance gave her agitation away.

Josh shifted from one foot to the other. "Ahh. Just saying. Now might not be the time to lose focus on the bouncing ball. You know-"

"I do know," Rebecca interrupted. "I know that every one of my big, macho, bad-ass brothers met and fell hard for their wives during a mission. I know that those lovey-dovey feelings took my brothers down for the count. Hard. Yet. Like myself, they still got their missions accomplished without incident. And I would really appreciate having the same considerations extended to me that all of you were given." Her tightly fisted hands rested on either side of her hip.

"Pfft, there were incidents," Josh scoffed. His waving hand circled inches from her face. "And, like, that's going to happen! Be real," he scolded. "You're my baby sister-"

"I'm almost twenty-eight years old. Not a baby." She poked him hard. The tip of her forefinger made contact with the middle of his forehead. "Whatever happened with Agent Collins, or is happening-"

"Happened? What the hell happened?!" Josh exploded.

Rebecca's hand waved wildly in front of her brother's face in the exact manner done to her mere moments before. "It doesn't matter!" she huffed. "Nothing is going to happen! We are agents on assignment only. I know where the ball is headed and have no intention of letting it get past me. Let the matter with Agent Collins go," she sighed solemnly. "I certainly have."

Tapping her watch, she added, "We don't have time for this, Josh." Her tone gentled, squeezing his arm. "I got this."

Josh hesitated for a few heartbeats. He closed his mouth and jerked his chin downward in reply but then swiftly added, "This isn't over. We'll discuss this later."

"Understood. When this mission gets completed, we can argue about it over the next Sunday dinner," Rebecca stepped back and stiffened her stance.

"Copy- you do as you are told when they arrive." Josh threw her a look that she deciphered to mean, 'I'm not fooling around about this.'

Shaking her head and sighing yet again, Rebecca walked out of the room.

****

Mr. Black contacted Jennifer Daniel's satellite phone on a secure line after sending her an anonymous email informing her of this unscheduled contact. As the call came through, she took a moment to steady her rapid breathing from the long trek between her private quarters and the small empty office she scouted out weeks ago in the Freedom compound.

"Good evening, Sir. You have information from Michael?"

"Yes. Nothing good. Sharpe and Nancy are making their move against the Maxwells. He's initiated Agent Patterson to her task. I'm unsure about the Patterson Brothers' next move regarding the child. MJ and Michael did locate a cell number from the Guardians Inc.'s moles. They hacked into the phone's carrier and intercepted a text communication from this... Mr. Pink. He is at the corporate facility and ready to take action. I need you at the Guardians Inc.'s Conshohocken site. He may lure Maxwell there."

Jennifer nodded her head before realizing Black couldn't see her. "Okay, Sir. But it will be a long shot. I'm hours away at most if I ride and forty minutes away if I get blades in the air."

"Don't make contact with Maxwell..." Mr. Black stated and thinking it through, added, "Or with anyone. Jennifer Daniels cannot be traced back to this mission.

"I'll make alternate plans in case we are too late. I'll find a way to get you at Freedom's site for longer periods. You'll be my eyes and ears when I'm not there. Hopefully, your suggestions will take root, and the Patterson Brothers will be en route. If Sharpe successfully takes them, that's where the Maxwells will go as well."

"I have no doubt the Pattersons have already organized a team of men in position to study the facility. Sean Patterson is as gifted in pursuing information through his hacking skills as William Maxwell before any special abilities come into play. He will pull on that thread the business card revealed and make the connection," Ms. Daniels confidently commented.

Black hesitated, knowing what he added next would surely raise her ire. But he couldn't help himself. "Jennifer don't take any unnecessary risks. If you get there and find, Sharpe or Johnson already there keep eyes on them and intervene only if Maxwell's life is in danger."

He almost grinned when he heard the muted sigh come over the line before her reply came through.

"I'm very good at my job, Sir. I know what to do," she reminded him.

"I'm well aware. Just don't get yourself injured. Michael will rip me a new one, and I'll pull you from this mission so fast, your head will spin."

There wasn't much of a surprise afterward when the call got disconnected without further comment from Jennifer Daniels.

Black's grin faded, replaced by a heavy frown. Things had just got critical, and he had to ensure he made the right moves. Or more people could get hurt other than just Black's enemies.

Would his...? Black clenched his jaw. *Would the FBI agent, Jeffery Collins, be there to keep Will Maxwell safe? Or does this agent have another agenda at play? And are Will Maxwell's abilities everything and more... than what I suspect?*

Mr. Black shook his head from side to side. *If their enemies got a hold of that kind of power, it would make my assignment that much more difficult.*

Either way, he needed them to survive this night because there were questions that required answers.

A battle was coming for them all.

Chapter Twenty-Nine

Allison had fallen asleep a little over an hour ago. Her breathing had turned soft and slow immediately after becoming horizontal. Will leaned on his side, chin resting on his open palm, and studied her as she dreamed. The peaceful expression she held in sleep soothed his thoughts considerably. He prayed that all of the plans they were making would pay off and that this madness would soon be over.

Hopefully, before then, he could squeeze in his minor omission about Allison's uncle, too. They hadn't gotten into details on when his company picked up her and Peggy McNeils' security detail. Not telling her that the bodyguards' supplied by Guardians, Inc. provided protection before they officially met at her uncle's Gala could cause issues. He needed time to smooth things over before he muddied the waters even more.

His cell phone started vibrating making a rattling sound on the table. Sitting up carefully, he reached for it. "Maxwell," he softly spoke into his device.

"Hey Will, it's Vincent. I hope I'm not interrupting, but this is important enough to call."

Will heard the urgency carried in his uncle's voice. "No. What's up?"

"I'm here at the office with your Dad; still working on the management transition, and I stumbled across some files that I think you need to see."

"Send them over... or I can just- "

"They're hard copies as well as electronic. They're related to some robberies of our older clients. And I don't want the risk of sending it out over email."

"Okay. Can't you get Dad and the security team to handle it?" He rubbed his hand through his hair, still watching Allison sleep.

"Well, I could, but the items stolen were Civil War artifacts, similar to your case."

Will slowly stood up so as not to shift the bed and disturb Allison. "How long ago?"

"Starting two years back and as recently as last month. What do you want me to do?"

"Ahh. I can be there in twenty." He disconnected the call, leaned over, and gently rubbed Allison's back. "Honey, wake up." It took a few attempts to shake her awake.

"Hmmm. What?" she slurred, dragging herself up from a deep sleep.

"Ally, I have to go," he reluctantly told her.

"It's time already?" She moved to get up.

"No. Stay. It hasn't been that long. I got a call from my uncle. It could be a lead. I have to take a look."

"What?" Allison rolled over and sat up. Her hair got smushed to one side and teased up in the back.

Leaning over her, Will played with some of the curls in disarray. *God, she is adorable.* He thought before continuing, "He found some lost files connected to the robberies"

"But how?"

"Not sure, but I have to go and find out." He picked up his jeans, put them on, and grabbed his jacket.

"Can I go with you?" she asked, already knowing what he would say.

He came to her side of the bed, leaned down to give her a quick but intense kiss, and then headed out. "No. I'll be too worried about you to do what needs doing."

She scooted off the bed and followed him, catching the tail end of Will's explanation to Jeff about Vincent's call.

"I'm going with you," Jeff insisted while tossing off the small throw.

"No. Stay here with Ally."

Jeff spotted Allison leaning against the kitchen island behind

Will's back. She shook her head adamantly from side to side and glared at Jeff. When she heard him say, "I'm still going." She held two thumbs up and nodded her head while biting her lower lip in agreement.

Allison came forward. "I'll be fine here. I'll sit tight and wait to hear from you or Jeff," she said while grabbing Will's hand. She silently pleaded with him to agree.

Will sighed in resignation. "Okay, fine. Come on then." He gestured at the door.

Jeff stretched and then shook his arms out. Getting right down to business, he rapidly fired information at Allison. "There is a car parked in the garage below. I'll give you the access code for the elevator. The keys are under the floor mat. Registration is in the glove compartment. You shouldn't need it, but it's there all the same."

Heading toward the leather satchel brought in earlier, Jeff pulled out the gun and ammunition, loaded it, and handed Allison the weapon with additional clips. "Will told me you'd had training. Don't hesitate to use it."

She nodded while setting the weapon on the counter. Her uncle had made sure she could handle several types of handguns and rifles. The iconic Browning Hi-Power semi-automatic Jeff gave her was one such model.

"Will, let's get the transmitter and activate it now. We'll leave it on from now on." Jeff left to retrieve it from the security room.

"Good idea," Will said as his gaze returned to Allison.

When returning, Jeff placed an incredibly small device on the counter. He rummaged through the kitchen drawer.

Allison ran her fingers over the small strip of adhesive backing that held the transmitter. It was the size of a small tick but flesh-colored instead of dark brown.

"A-ha!" Jeff's voice resonated in the open space. Allison's eyes lifted from the device to see what the excitement was all about.

Pulling out a small tube and a pair of tweezers, Jeff gestured for Will to get closer. When Will tilted his head sideways, Jeff dabbed a drop of the glue behind his ear. Pulling the transmitter off its backing, he pressed the device onto the dab of glue and kept the pressure on it. It didn't take long at all for the bond to dry properly.

"This should remain secure for about two days, at least. It's like superglue but stronger. Keep checking it and reapply if necessary." He handed Will the tube.

The small container got tucked into the shaft of Will's boot.

"Let's go, Allison," Jeff instructed. "Follow us out, and I'll give you the security codes to write down." He rummaged through the drawer again and pulled out a notepad and pen, handing them to her. He used his hip to slam the drawer closed, and then they all headed out.

It took under five minutes to coordinate the security codes and operating procedures.

"Ally, you have the backup speed dial numbers in case of an emergency," Jeff reminded her as the perimeter gate opened to let them pull their bikes through.

Will pulled her tight to his chest. The gentle, circular rub on her back did nothing to soothe her racing heart. His mouth got close to her right ear. "Try to get some rest, Ally. This case will be cracked wide open by the end of tomorrow. I can take some time off and hide somewhere private and secluded. We'll take a real honeymoon."

"With Sara?" Allison tilted her chin up, and met his adoring gaze, and spotted the grin that flashed on his lips.

He nodded once and shrugged. "I guess it won't be a traditional honeymoon-"

"No. It won't. But it will be perfect for us," Allison assured him.

The once-waffling bride now stood absolutely determined to break away from the fears holding her back from what she truly wanted. And what she truly wanted was Will and her family to remain together.

She sent her thoughts to Will while mouthing silently, *I Love you. Be safe.*

"I love you too. You stay put." Will nodded again. His grip tightened briefly before dropping his arms and stepping away. His strides took him to Jeff's side. The gates closed, separating the two areas.

Allison nodded and raised her hand with thumbs up beyond the locked gate.

Will and Jeff both lowered their chin in confirmation, closed their helmet visors, revved their bikes' engines, and took off down the road.

Allison slowly walked back inside in heavy contemplation. The tranquil setting of the nearby water bubbling over rocks could not soothe the worry chasing her thoughts. But worry wasn't productive.

If Vincent Maxwell's lead helped shed light on some answers, it was worth checking it out. Finding solutions, no matter how slight the puzzle piece turned out, still got them closer to viewing the whole picture.

She was beginning to understand that her uncle's dream-linked talks made a lot of things clear. She needed to stop pushing people away and start forming stronger alliances. It was becoming evident that worry wasn't a useful enterprise to get caught up in.

Her pace toward the building increased with the deliberate extraction of fear striving to hold her down and make her powerless.

She didn't want to be powerless.

She wanted to be part of a team. And that team needed everything she had to give. Allison wouldn't fail them again. They would search every nook and cranny to determine the proper course forward.

Because they desperately needed answers to defeat the Sons of Liberty and Copperhead's threats against their loved ones. And Allison wanted to be among the group that saw it happen.

Chapter Thirty

"Let's move out," James Patterson called to his younger sibling.

Lia, James' wife, hugged her husband and gave him a quick kiss on the lips. "Be safe. Give me a shout when you are settled in." She tapped her temple, knowing he'd communicate with her through their personal telepathic link.

I love you. Came through loud and clear in her mind. His open palm rested on his wife's rounded belly. A loving pat expressed more than words could say.

Brian Patterson nodded, preparing to leave. He gave his wife, Jeanine, a quick, passionate kiss.

"Remember your promise. I get the scoop on whatever is happening at this National Park?" she joked while curtailing her daughter's exploration of the fuzzy caterpillar moving across their path. She laughed when she spied on her husband's eye roll. "Be safe, my love," she said. Stepping back, she and Lia attempted to corral their young charges back inside.

James watched his family make their way inside Frank Marshall's gated estate. His former commander and his wife, Jenna, would do everything humanly possible to keep them all safe.

In order to do his job, James had to seal that mental compartment up tight.

Leaving for a mission never got any easier. But James and his brothers couldn't be anything else than what they were. And it's a good thing they have partners who accept and love that part of them.

"I found us a good route. It won't buy us much in time saved. Maybe some, but not a lot, but it will more than make up for the annoying traffic around Washington DC."

"Copy," James replied. "Sean is shadowing Rebecca. The team they sent to Maxwell's safehouse is secured. Allison's family is en route to another location. The Copperhead agents are neutralized and won't be reporting anything back we don't want sent. We're clear on that front. We just have to monitor where they send Rebecca. My gut tells me this Freedman's Village is the key." James stole a quick look away from the road to meet his brother's gaze.

Brian nodded. His fingers rapidly tapped his thigh.

"What?" James prompted.

"That's if we aren't walking into a trap. How can you be sure that this Jennifer Daniels isn't setting us up?" Brian asked.

"Because my gut tells me otherwise," James replied.

"Your gut has been known to be incorrect... occasionally. Remember, Michelle Robinson. You read that whole situation wrong." His smirk reflected his enjoyment of pointing out this particular mistake.

"Fuck!" James sighed. "You all are never gonna let me forget that either." He smirked back, sharing in on the family joke. "Still, it all worked out," he pointed out, referring to his and Lia's marriage and growing family.

His brother grinned before turning away. When his gaze slid back around, it held a more serious note. "Seriously, James. I hope you've hit the nail on this. I'm not so much worried we can't get out of a sticky situation..."

James glanced over and met his brother's gaze. Brian sighed. "If we're wrong about this place, we don't have much else to follow. They could take the Maxwells almost anywhere."

The oldest Patterson brother turned back to keep his focus on the road. What his brother just said was what they were all thinking. It wasn't 'if' they grabbed the Maxwells anymore, but when they got to them. Their plan for managing the situation counted on many factors holding true.

The biggest one was where their youngest sister would be ending up. It didn't sit well with him leaving her in the Sons of

Liberty's company for long.

"She had a chance to take us out," James murmured. "Back at Guardians, Inc.'s facility. Ms. Daniels could have done more than enough damage. Why sedate Sean and me?" he asked.

Brian shook his head. "No bodies to hide?" he answered. A heavy sigh escaped. "It takes effort to kill someone."

"Not if they inject something into one's bloodstream," James answered. "There could have been a multitude of drugs used. But they used ones that were fast-acting, non-lethal, and quick to dissipate. She had motive, means, and opportunity. And why leave behind the card?"

A loud ping of an incoming communication interrupted the brainstorming. James brought his phone up so he could read the notification—unknown number.

He swiped across the screen to activate the app. His eyes scanned the text.

"And my gut tells me her agenda is currently aligned with ours," he stated, angling his phone out for his brother to read the screen.

The short text message solidified James Patterson's theory on Jennifer Daniels.

If I miscalculated the Amazing Patterson Brothers' capabilities, I'm going to be royally pissed. You need to BE THERE now! - JD

****

Senator Phillip J. Buchanan paced from one length of the formal foyer to the next. His shoes clicked against the checkered styled black and white marble flooring. The opulent decor surrounding him went unnoticed.

Why should he care about anything in this mausoleum when he had no voice during its acquisition?

The purchase of this property was forced on him. And just because his name was on the deed didn't mean it was his to do with what he wanted.

The Sons of Liberty were the actual owners of this residence.

The reflective glimmering from the massive chandelier above coated his handsome features as if the rays were drawn to him by the turbulent energy vibrating from his frame.

Darkness always needed light to eradicate it.

And Phillip Buchanan had his share of darkness sucking the light out of his soul. It weighed on him fiercely.

His enemies were getting closer to the secret he had held tight to his heart for decades. Only the clear-headed would stand a chance of defeating them this time around. He pushed down the frustration that wanted to escape.

He would have to play his part perfectly–in this dangerous cat-and-mouse game–or Allison's life could be forfeited.

His pledge to Sara Marie Buchanan, Allison's mother, could not fall short of the mark.

"I have too many sins piled on to stop now," he said softly into the empty room, not caring that the bugs planted throughout the house would pick up his spoken words. They would misinterpret them, and that worked better for his cause.

However, wrong their assumptions, he wasn't like the many other political associates who were coerced or bribed to help the Sons of Liberty's agenda. He took this opportunity to better another, more important cause. But Allison's knowledge of this reason couldn't see the light of day for some time.

She wasn't ready. Yet.

The realization that he could forfeit her forgiveness if he continued this path weighed on him. But sometimes, things weren't black and white. And there were many levels of gray to get lost within.

Senator Buchanan knew this more than most, and he had no problem diving into those murky pools in order to protect his family.

He only hoped that once the true purpose lay clear, Allison would understand why they hid the truths under so many secrets.

Allison believed in their family curse. A belief Phillip did well to foster within her at a young, impressionable age. Because she wasn't entirely wrong in that worry; Allison just got the vital part of the curse incorrect.

"That, too, was my fault," he whispered.

The Buchanan curse wasn't about death stalking their loved ones. However, tragedies did fall upon those they very deeply cared about.

Senator Buchanan sighed in pain. His heart skipped a beat, remembering that loss.

Allison's mother sacrificed everything to ensure her daughter stayed safe from the curse. There wasn't a day that went by that he didn't wish for the chance to go back in time and do things differently.

Maybe then, his heartache would heal.

"But to what end?" Phillip softly probed.

Because The Buchanan curse wasn't about death stalking them at all; the curse was about power.

Unlimited power.

And the Buchanan bloodline had it running in their veins. Tenfold.

Allison's fear of her loved ones getting hurt by the proximity to her has a layer of truth. But it had more to do with what power-hungry people would do to get to her birthright.

Or, more importantly, when the power in her blood was

released; what matters of afflictions could be possible?

The power keg unleashed could destroy this world.

The End

Guardians, Inc. Series- Part 2

Excerpt of Resilient Hearts-

Book 3 in the Guardians, Inc. series

Jennifer Daniels had arrived too late.

Nothing could be done now except keep her eyes on the situation and provide damage control if things went sideways.

As Edward Sharpe's administrative assistant–for one of the higher-ups within the Sons of Liberty–this failure would usually come with unpleasant consequences. She had enough bruises already from Sharpe's bad-tempered backlashes along her upper arms and shoulders.

However, those physical discomforts were the least of her concerns. For tonight, her role varied significantly from what Edward Sharpe could even imagine.

The calm focus and experienced eyes of Mr. Black's hired agent observed as Will Maxwell and Jeffrey Collins drove by her a few moments ago.

No one paid her any mind. She did well to blend into the surrounding shadows, with her appearance mimicking the non-descript gray sedan she sat within. Her mousy-colored hair in a tight bun only highlighted her unassuming facial features. And the clothes she wore–purposely chosen to discourage anyone from giving her a second look–hid her body shape.

She glanced at her watch and assumed the trap had been set already. A murmur from behind got her attention, and she turned away from the back security gate. The guard she accosted moments ago lay against the back seat. His hands and feet secured with zip-ties, and a cloth was placed between his lips, wrapped around his head and fastened in the back.

"Yes. I know. A mere female, as unaspiring as myself, got the drop on big, strong you. But..." Her gaze went to the badge she brought closer to see before adding, "Mr. Radley, be assured that many have tried before you and have failed."

Her head swiveled back to look out from the windshield. Her fingers drummed against the soft leather of the steering wheel. The rotating team, including the guard presently resting in her backseat, made intersecting points along the site's perimeter.

The street lamps' illumination couldn't get through the car's tinted window.

Within the darkened interior of the vehicle, Jennifer Daniels absentmindedly added, "Although I'm not what you may consider the 'Good Guy...' I'm not quite the bad one either. So don't go worrying about your boss on my account." With eyes closed, she centered her mind and activated her incredible ability.

The tied-up guard rapidly blinked his eyes as a shimmering light went off within the darkness, like several flashes from a camera with a sub-par bulb. By the time his vision adjusted to the sudden illumination, the returning darkness followed afterward just as quickly.

But he did catch the sound of the driver's door open and close.

His angle of sight was compromised due to his location. But, as a figure stepped to the side of the car, the captive guard blinked his eyes several times, not believing what his vision showed.

He could have sworn that a duplication of himself just moved away from the car.

The beating in his chest sped up once more. This time, in fear for the slim-figured woman with the soft voice. Worrying about her meeting up with his doppelganger to get inside the building didn't make sense.

Why did he fear for this unknown woman?

Especially after she got the jump on him and tied him up in the backseat of this car, and it didn't go unnoticed that the car that held him captive was most likely stolen.

For some unknown reason, the female stranger didn't come off to him as bad. He just knew she was there to help.

He shook his head in bemusement at that notion. Even knowing that when he told everyone what happened, they would think him nuts.

****

Jeff stepped out first from the elevator, and Will followed close behind.

The main executive boardroom stood to the right, with two medium-sized conference rooms directly across from the elevator doors. A hallway to the left led to a separate suite with additional meeting rooms, department heads' executive offices and the Department of Human Resources.

The interior decor of this level, along with the high-ranking executive offices one floor above, featured light wood tones with recessed panel wainscoting, decorative floor, base molding, and ceiling cornice trim throughout. Also, tastefully decorated custom silk wallpaper and plush neutral carpeting provided an understated elegance meant for an impressive first impression.

Jeff held out his hand, pausing Will's approach farther into the suite. He allowed his abilities to open fully and scanned the area. When Jeff could not sense any violent energy or any nearby occupants, he slowly rounded the corner to their left.

With the suite's double-door entrance resting open, they spotted the Senator's security personnel standing guard just beyond.

As Jeff's gun got tucked into the back of his jeans, he signaled for Will to follow him. A loud conversation could be heard as they got closer. Will and Jeff greeted the Senator's secret service agent, flanking the door, and walked into the private administrative area. They immediately saw two members of Will's family through the fully glazed conference room partition, which was centered between two larger meeting areas.

Will's uncle, Vincent Maxwell, sat at the conference table. Will's dad leaned down behind his younger sibling, reviewing the laptop computer screen. In the back of the room, another secret service agent stood in position.

Both Maxwells turned when they heard Will and Jeff's arrival. With similar builds, the brothers both had brown hair and light blue eyes. Their rounded facial features matched as well, but Vincent Maxwell had a sharper jawline than his brother.

Senator Maxwell stood an inch taller than Vincent at six-foot, two. His stance held authority and confidence that his brother's bearing had always lacked.

Instead, Vincent's demeanor held a nervous energy that prevented him from standing still. Even now, his fingers tapped on the tabletop at a fast-driven pace.

Will's dad headed toward his son. He grabbed Will up in a tight bear hug before swiftly composing himself into a calm, steady demeanor. It was a mannerism he had developed when dealing with the most harried situations in Congress. "You shouldn't be here, son," he scolded Will in a gruff tone. "I told Vincent not to call you."

With the transition of executive positions, the call should have been made by the new COO of Will's company, Senator James Maxwell. A position the younger Maxwell brother, Vincent, had held before.

But as talks of buying out his nephew began to circulate, and Will had no desire to sell his company, a change grew necessary. And as luck would have it, retiring from his governmental position, Will's dad provided a much needed solution.

This shifting leadership looked to agree with all parties involved. At least, that was what the father and son had believed.

But they couldn't have been more wrong.

"It's okay Dad, I need to see the files to get an idea of what we're dealing with. It could be related to this whole mess."

The retired Senator pivoted to Jeff and pulled him into another tight but quick embrace. "I hope you're taking proper care of my son and yourself," Senator Maxwell said while stepping back and looking over them both in great detail. It had been almost a year since he got to see the two young men in person.

Videoconferencing meetings and phone calls just didn't feel the same.

Jeff assumed he and Will must have passed inspection because the Senator nodded sharply before gesturing for them both to the table. Jeff caught a fleeting look sent between the Senator and his most trusted bodyguard.

The guard acknowledged his understanding with a tiny but significant nod. The guard's demeanor changed from relaxed professional to seasoned combatant from one moment to the next.

Will addressed his uncle with warm greetings, "Evening Uncle. Congrats on picking up Havard campuses' contract. You've really taken the school dormitory subsidiary division to new heights."

Vincent nodded back and gave him a good-natured slap on the shoulder. "Your good name and contacts opened the doors. I'm confident other campuses with dorm living will come on board soon." He turned toward the table and pointed to the stack of files laid out on the conference table and the stored data files on the laptop. "Let's dive right in, and maybe we'll get you something you can use."

It wasn't long before they all could see the pattern unfold amidst the files and the robberies.

Each case reflected a client using a system from Will's company for mid-level security, and when better software technology became available, they got the recommended upgrades needed.

However, beginning two years ago, each scheduled upgrade from specific clients having Civil War collections showed their service had been canceled within weeks of their planned upgrades. Each client had requested that all their client information be transferred to a competitor's product and service. Someone in Will's company had followed through with this request each time.

This was strictly against Guardians, Inc.'s policy.

And Will had a very bad feeling sink to his stomach.

This could mean only one thing.